Green and Pleasant Land

David Flin

Book 1 in the Building Jerusalem series.

First published by Sergeant Frosty Publications 2021

Copyright © 2021 David Flin

All rights reserved.

Cover artwork by Anastasia Nikolova

For further Books from
Sergeant Frosty Publications, please visit:

www.sergeantfrosty.com

Dedicated to:
My son, Andrew.
You make me very proud.

Green and Pleasant Land

His father had been furious. His father hadn't understood, hadn't even tried to understand. There had been threats, talk of disgrace to the family name, and promises of bribes if he were to drop the idea.

"Where did you get this damn fool notion from?" he had asked over dinner.

Thomas couldn't explain. He had tried, but his father hadn't understood. "There's no danger any more. Everything is so, so arranged. Go to school, make contacts, get prepared for managing the estate, find a suitable wife who will be a credit to the family, eventually take over running the estate, and prepare my sons to take over from me when it's my turn to go. That's my life for the next 50 years. No challenge, no danger, no risk, no excitement, no hard work, no sense of satisfaction of beating the odds. Just mind-numbing tedious predictability."

"It's a girl, isn't it? You've got some servant girl into trouble. I know you get on well with servants and animals. Still, we can pay her off. It's not as though that class can't be bought off. It's not like we haven't done it before."

"There's no girl, Father. Just boredom."

"But the Army? You want to wear the Uniform of Honour?" His father had been disbelieving, almost contemptuous. "Don't you remember your trip to the State school?"

"Perfectly, Father." That was true. He remembered standing at the entrance, puzzled by the Board of Honour. It was out of keeping with the school. The school was run-down. It wasn't old, but it was well-worn and cheaply built and in need of repair. Peeling paint, mismatched windows, doors that had warped with the weather. Too many people, not enough repair and maintenance. Everything done cheaply. Everything except this one board. Solid enduring stone, with name after name after name carefully engraved on it. After each name was a place and a date.

"That's what State schools are for," his father had explained. "We give them an education, look after them, feed them, house them, spend taxes on them. No orphan or any child from the underclass goes hungry or wants for the necessities of life. In return, they give service. They are the ones who wear the Uniform of Honour." He had almost spat out the words. "For such as them, the uniform is an honour."

Thomas remembered watching as another name was added to the wall. "Graduated?" he had asked one of the older school children.

"No, Sir. Fallen. Skirmish out in Persia." The boy had been cautious but respectful, eyes carefully blank. Just like those of a wary animal, unsure whether you intended it harm or not.

"So, it's not for those who have graduated?"

"Oh no, Sir. Well, they've graduated, but it's for them what's died in Service."

When Thomas had got home, he'd read in the paper about an incident in Persia, disruptive rebels with German backing. There weren't many details, just one of the usual bits of troublemaking in one of the corners of the Empire. Rebels had tried to disrupt the oil supply, and Persian forces had been flown in behind them, cut off their lines of retreat, and eliminated them. "One of our airships failed to return. Some casualties were taken."

Thomas had tried to imagine what it had been like. The excitement, the fear. Doing something. Doing something that meant something to other people. That was the moment when he began to feel dissatisfied with his lot in life.

"It's quite simple," his father had explained. "The Army is a Service. It is for the serving class. We run things, and they serve us. That's how things are meant to be." His father had then explained how he would never fit into the Army. "You are not a servant. No matter how easily you can talk to them, you are not one of them. You could no more spend your time always surrounded by them, live with them, than you could with your hounds or your horses."

For some time, Thomas had said nothing. He'd sneaked back to the State school and watched. The children seemed vibrant and alive. The children he knew were, well, soft. Indolent. Spoilt. They wanted for nothing and they were soft. These children weren't.

He'd tricked his father. He said that he was going to spend some time in Paris and he hinted at a possible business deal.

"Be very careful. The French are an immoral lot. Not cruel. They're not German. But their morals are, lax."

He hadn't gone to Paris. He'd gone to the State school. He gave £10 to the headmaster and arranged to teach history for a term. He'd sent letters to a friend in Paris, who had sent them on to his father, to maintain the deception.

It was a strange time. The other teachers were middle-class, of course. Worthy professionals, for the most part, imparting a sense of duty and discipline into the children of the underclass. He became friends with some of the teachers, including Mrs Hunter, a nurse whose husband was away for a long time on a sea voyage.

He'd watched the children at sport, and he'd noticed how they played the games. They were fair and they followed the rules, but they were hard. He'd idly wondered how they would fare against a real school. Not that any such match would ever be arranged.

Their knowledge of history before the Franco-Prussian war was lamentable. He'd asked them about the Heptarchy, and they hadn't even known what that was, never mind any details. They'd known much more about modern history, although they saw it in an odd manner. The growing tensions between the powers, the constant manoeuvres and sponsoring of disruptive elements in the sphere of influence of the other, the skirmishes here and there. They viewed it as squabbles over turf, and they didn't appreciate the underlying political situations.

They'd heard of disruptive philosophies, intended to disturb the lower orders. None of them knew much about the details, and they accepted their lot in life. "That's the deal, ain't it, Sir. We graft. Them as understand these things work out how we graft."

Thomas had agreed, but that wasn't quite right. They certainly grafted, and the boys went into the Army or the mines or wherever they were needed. But were the decisions about how and where and why they grafted, and often died, made properly?

He didn't know what his students had learned from him, but he learned a lot from them. His father never suspected a thing.

That had all led to this decision and his father was furious. He'd threaten to disown him if he did join the Army. His father didn't make threats lightly; he knew that he meant it. Dinner was finished in an angry silence.

The next morning, he packed a bag with his own possessions. He made sure he had nothing that he hadn't bought himself. He had no idea what the future would bring, but it would be his own future, not his family's.

*****

Joining the Army had been childishly simple. He'd spent a long time coming up with a story and a new name, making sure it made sense, but didn't look too perfect.

"Thomas O'Grady?" said the sergeant in the recruiting office. "You don't sound Irish."

"I'm not Irish, Sir." The sir was a good touch, Thomas thought. "Family came over during the famine. Trying to get to America, but they ran out of money."

"You say you're good with horses?"

"Very good," he'd said. "Grew up with horses, Sir."

"And you want to join the cavalry? Why do you want to join the Army?"

"Honourable job, Sir. Get to do my duty, see the world, adventure, Sir."

The sergeant had just snorted. "Why do you want to join the Army? In trouble, are you?"

Thomas had paused. Everything he'd been told was that the Army was an honourable job for the serving classes. Hard and dangerous work, but well-paid and doing duty for the good of the country.

"Come on, lad. It'll all come out, but the Army looks after its own."

"Got a girl in trouble," Thomas said. It was the first thing that came into his mind. It had been the first thing his father had said.

"And?" The sergeant obviously expected more.

"Above my station, Sir. Her father wasn't happy."

"Sign on, and you can be rid of that problem."

It was that easy. He'd asked for a posting to a cavalry regiment, explaining that he knew about horses. He'd been sent to the First Battalion of the Rifle Brigade.

The training had been strange. It had been both very easy and hard. After drill and route marching, they'd spent hour after hour on the firing range, practising relentlessly five rounds rapid fire. Sergeant Taylor was in charge of them, and he expected them to hit a three-inch target at a hundred yards five times out of five in fifteen seconds.

When they started, Thomas would have said it was impossible. But it turned out that practise made perfect. It also made for a very sore shoulder. The Lee-Enfield had a hefty kick to it.

On the other hand, the training was easy because no-one seemed to expect recruits to think or know anything very much. They were just cogs in a machine. There was a constant stream of petty regulations that appeared to have no point, but he quickly learned not to ask their training sergeant the reason why.

"Rifleman Recruit So-Called O'Grady wants to know why. Riflemen don't need to know why. They gets told what to do, and they does it, and that's an end to the matter."

"Ours not to reason why, ours but to do or die, Sergeant?"

That had been a mistake. Sergeant Taylor had kept his eye on Thomas after that. "Got it in one, Rifleman Recruit So-Called O'Grady."

What was worse was that the nickname So-Called stuck, and the others in his training platoon used that name for him. He told himself that it could have been worse.

But the hardest part of the training was the never-ending drill. The other recruits had been in corps at their State schools, and they knew the basics of drill. His school didn't have a corps. It would have been a waste of time. Sergeant Taylor had not been slow to point out Thomas' shortcomings.

His buddy in the platoon showed him the basics in their few moments of free time. A swarthy, scarred little man, Sicilian, he said. His name was Francesco Barrilaro, and the Army changed his name to Barry, and the platoon called him Frank.

When the platoon had first been shown their hut, there were bunk beds, and they'd each been allocated one. It had been explained to them that each pair in a bunk were responsible for each other. If one got into trouble, they both got punished. One for getting into trouble, and the other for letting him. So, Frank taught Thomas drill, and Thomas taught Frank English, and they became buddies.

The rest of the platoon quickly realised Thomas wasn't from their class. They seemed to shrug and accept it, which puzzled him. Frank had explained.

"It like that rhyme. Rich man, poor man, beggar man, thief. It not matter. You are Rifleman now. What you were not important. What you will be not important. All that important is what you are."

Sergeant Taylor did not agree that they were Riflemen. He explained to them that they were recruits, and of less military value than the Colonel's peacocks.

The recruits hated those peacocks. They screeched and squawked at night, and they received the best of attention. When the hot weather came, the recruits had to erect shade for the peacocks. Voluntarily, and in their own time, of course. Sergeant Taylor had detailed off those who he had decided were volunteers.

They hated those peacocks, but it was the peacocks that gave Thomas his first chance for advancement.

The Colonel had heard that there were foxes in the neighbourhood. He arranged for guards to be posted around the clock to protect the peacocks.

The first night, a peacock went missing, and the soldiers on guard were berated for their laxity. The same thing happened on the second night, and the third.

On the fourth night, Thomas, Frank, and two others who had incurred the displeasure of Sergeant Taylor were on guard duty.

"It not a fox," said Frank. "They taken for pot."

"I've got an idea," said Thomas. If there was one thing he'd learned from his father, it was how to hunt foxes. And he'd spent some time talking with their gamekeeper about foxes.

Leaving the other two to guard the peacocks, Thomas and Frank had snuck out of camp to the nearby woods. They were recruits, and they didn't realise just how much trouble they would be in if they got caught. Fortunately for them, they weren't. In the woods, Thomas looked around for signs of a fox burrow, and was quickly successful in this. Thomas lit a fire, and put damp leaves on it to make smoke, and drove the smoke into the burrow. This caused the fox to rush out and Frank was able to grab it.

Thomas had wanted to take the fox alive back to present in the morning, but it quickly became obvious that the fox was having none of this. Frank solved the problem with a single stroke from his knife.

Come the morning, Sergeant Taylor came to check on them. Sure enough, a peacock had been taken, but Thomas and Frank were able to present the culprit.

The Sergeant had not been impressed. The Colonel, however, was. "Shame about the one he got, but that should be an end to this. They did well, Sergeant."

"If you say so, Sir."

Thomas suspected that Sergeant Taylor knew the truth.

"How did you catch it?" the Colonel asked.

It was a direct question. Thomas had to answer. "We're Riflemen, Sir. Riflemen on guard. No-one or nothing gets past us. Sergeant Taylor taught us, Sir."

"Well done, Sergeant. Excellent work."

Later, Sergeant Taylor confiscated the peacock. Such is the way with Sergeants.

*****

It had taken a while, but Thomas had taught Frank the fundamentals of bridge. That meant that with Peter and young Windy, they had a four. Not that they had a great deal of free time, but since as recruits they were confined to barracks until they were trained, they were able to find some time.

You could learn a lot about someone by the way that they played bridge. Peter, Rifleman Recruit Grant, was confident, sometimes overbold with his bidding, and very precise and accurate in his play. He was older than most of the other recruits and he was a dab-hand at fixing things. He was also more knowledgeable than most and was easily the best recruit at drill. He had been the one who had been adamant that they didn't play for money and referred to money as being outmoded and the scourge of the masses. He got angry with authority, and this often got him into trouble with the sergeant. Thomas suspected that there was a hidden story behind this. It was, however, understood that one didn't ask why someone had joined.

With young Windy, you didn't need to ask. He volunteered the information. He was so obviously underage, but he was desperate to stay. He was a clever lad. Very clever. Scholarship material, until his father had been killed in a factory accident. Slim, and with almost delicate features, but tougher than he looked. He was the oldest of five children, so it was up to him to be the breadwinner of the family. The Army sent his pay to his family, and he made the best of the situation. His cautious bidding balanced that of his buddy. The two of them got on well.

"If I ever see a farthing change hands, you boys will feel my displeasure," said Sergeant Taylor from the doorway of the hut. "Riflemen Recruits Barry, Grant, Miller, O'Grady. Lieutenant Hawkins wants a word with you. You've been chosen from a host of volunteers for a special honour."

"Sergeant, we haven't volunteered for anything."

"Wrong, Rifleman Recruit Miller. You volunteered the day that you signed up. The rest is just details over exactly what it was you volunteered for."

"But Sergeant," Windy continued.

"Lad, a volunteer is someone what misunderstood the question."

There was no arguing with a Sergeant, and with no further ado, the four of them were taken to see their Lieutenant.

Lieutenant Hawkins sat at a desk in his quarters, working on some papers. Older than most of the other junior officers, he was a square-jawed, burly man who walked with a bit of a limp. The recruits speculated about that limp, but the Lieutenant never spoke about it.

All that the recruits knew was that he was old, in his early 30s, the other Lieutenants didn't treat him quite the same, and that he was a stickler for getting the basics right.

The four stood at attention in front of his desk while he continued to write slowly and carefully. He finally finished, and carefully put the pen away.

"Stand at ease," he said in a soft voice. "Riflemen Recruits Barry, Grant, Miller, and O'Grady. You've come to the attention of the Colonel." He paused, letting the enormity sink in. "The Colonel has noticed lowly riflemen recruits. He's specifically asked for you for a job. I'm going to have to rely on you not to let the platoon down. Sergeant Taylor, make sure that these four are smartly dressed for the job."

Sergeant Taylor wasn't pleased at this, but he kept his face impassive.

Lieutenant Hawkins looked at the four recruits. They'd learned to wait rather than asking questions. They would be told soon enough.

"The Colonel has said that because of your good work in guarding the peacocks, and ensuring the culprit was caught and protecting the rest of the flock, he's got a treat for you. O'Grady, you have something to say?"

"Ostentation, Sir."

"Actually, your reward will involve that, but I don't think that's what you meant."

"It's an ostentation of peacocks, Sir."

"Rather appropriate. I'm sure the Colonel will be fascinated. Anyway, the Colonel has decided to reward you by selecting you to be mess servants at the Officers' Mess Dinner tonight. Let you see a bit of luxury."

Each of the four had the same thought. Their reward was to be given extra work in a situation where making the slightest mistake, or even just being there when an officer or a guest got annoyed for no reason, could lead to dire consequences. Watching other people eat and drink and dance. They weren't convinced this was much of a reward.

After a pause to allow these thoughts to sink in, the Lieutenant went on. "If you do the job to my satisfaction, then I will see to it that you will be able to dispose of the leftover food. That is if you do the job to my satisfaction. Sergeant, make sure that they are presentable."

*****

Sergeant Taylor was resplendent in his dress uniform, keeping a discrete eye on the guests to the Officers' Mess Dinner, and keeping an unsubtle eye on the four recruits. The RSM was an even more imposing figure, for all that he was not much more than five and one-half feet tall. He somehow seemed taller.

The attention of the recruits was on the table, which was replete with silver and bejewelled tokens taken in campaigns from the White House to Casablanca, from Coruna to Cawnpore, from Ladysmith to Lofoten, from Bogota to Baghdad. All place names on the regiment's battle honours, all of them forgotten outside the Army, except to a few dedicated, specialist historians.

Peter snorted. "When officers do it, they call it Spoils of War, and it gets pride of place. When soldiers do it, they call it looting and punish you for it. It's the constant injustice of the ruling classes."

The regular Mess servants had glared at the four of them. The Mess servants couldn't complain. The Colonel had given the order. They couldn't complain, but they could make the four know they were unwelcome, and they would certainly not help them out. This was not where Riflemen should be, and certainly not mere recruits.

It was a Guest Dinner. Officers from another regiment had been invited, and other guests. It was important, and the Mess Sergeant certainly wasn't going to let outsiders serve food to the officers and guests. They might take liberties.

Which left the four with the menial task of looking after coats and clearing up debris and just being useful and hoping that it would soon come to an end.

"You're new to this," said a well-dressed middle-aged lady as she handed a coat to Thomas. She had a slight American accent.

Since it wasn't a question, as such, Thomas said nothing. It seemed the safest thing to do.

"Probably wisest," the lady said. "Garnet said that he'd arranged for new guards to be here. You must be one of the people who saved his precious peacocks."

"Yes, Ma'am."

"Hateful creatures. I doubt that the other soldiers thanked you. I've got a job for you. Two jobs, in fact. Possibly a third."

"Yes, Ma'am." There was nothing else he could say to the Colonel's lady.

"Firstly, our car was not running properly on the way here. Garnet insists that there's nothing wrong with it. I believe that there is. He boasted about your initiative, so I expect it to be fixed when we leave. I'm sure you can arrange that."

"Yes, Ma'am," said Thomas, despondently. He knew nothing about cars. On the other hand, Peter fixed things, maybe he knew something about cars.

"Initiative, remember? If mechanics fix cars, it can't be that difficult. Secondly, Garnet. Colonel Dalkeith to you. He is in one of his moods, and he's going to get this regiment into difficulty by boasting to Dicky, that's Major-General Younghusband, and Teddie, that's Colonel de Villiers. I expect you to make sure Garnet, Colonel Dalkeith, doesn't get too badly drunk. I don't much care how you do it, and Dicky and Teddie can get as drunk as they like, but I expect Garnet to be no more than merry when we leave. Understood?" She gave a little half-smile, but Thomas couldn't work out what that was about.

"Yes, Ma'am." Thomas was beginning to wonder if he would ever get to say anything else.

"Finally, Garnet has come up with a wonderful scheme for after-dinner entertainment. A scavenger hunt. You will assist my team, and I expect to win. Is that understood? Scavenging is a very important part of being a soldier. Now, repeat back to me what it is I require of you."

"Yes, Ma'am. One, fix the Colonel's car. Two, keep the Colonel from getting intoxicated. Three, assist your team in taking part in a scavenger hunt."

"Winning a scavenger hunt," the Colonel's lady said sharply. "I can't abide nearly or almost or second place. Winning, that's what people remember, and that's what I require."

"Permission to ask a question, Ma'am." When the Colonel's lady nodded, Thomas continued. "Why me?"

"Because I'm an interfering busybody of a dragon who has seen enough soldiers to know which have potential for advancement. Your name is?"

"Rifleman Recruit O'Grady, Ma'am."

"O'Grady? Really? Was that the best you could come up with?"

"Yes, Ma'am."

****

"She wants me to fix her car?" Peter was incredulous. "She doesn't give us orders. She's not in the Army. I'm not doing it."

"If you can't do it, say so, Peter."

"It's not that I *can't* do it. It's that I *won't* do it. I'm not getting my uniform filthy dirty for no Capitalist not even in the Regiment, not for all the tea in Timbuctoo."

"Capitalist?"

"There's loads of officers' wives who think soldiers are just servants who exist to do things for them. Never any payment, so it's slavery, not servant. Officers are bad enough. Officers' wives? The worst."

Thomas was interested. "You were in the Army before?"

Peter glowered. "REME. Seven years. Then I left, went into the repair business. I fixed things. Worked hard, saved every penny I had and started up me own business. Had loads of work, but too many of them just didn't pay from one month to the next. That put me into debt, and bang goes me business. So here I am again."

"That's a shame." Thomas didn't really know what to say. He'd never really needed to think about money before. It was just something you had. "You tell her you won't do it." There was no way Thomas was going to.

Ten minutes later, Thomas glanced outside. Peter was looking at the engine of the Colonel's car.

The Mess Servants made sure Thomas and the other recruits got nowhere near actually serving at the table. That meant that Thomas didn't have much to do other than stand around. As the officers and guests ate, Thomas noticed something about the junior officers. There were two different types of junior officer.

There was the young and self-confident type, who had an air of casual entitlement, and who treated the Mess Servants as just part of the furniture. Spotless and exquisite and expensive uniforms.

The other type was older, quieter, listening more than they spoke. Their eyes were constantly moving, trying to watch everything. Most of them wore uniforms that were well-kept, but older, with some signs of repairs.

"Gentlemen and Players," Thomas thought. He talked with Frank about the next task. Keeping the Colonel sober, or at least, not letting him get too drunk.

"I have idea," said Frank. "Sicilian whisky. You explain, I serve."

"Explain what? How is this going to work? What is Sicilian whisky?"

"I serve three. Two have Scotch whisky, one has watered whisky."

"But the colour will be different."

"Not with water I use."

Thomas shook his head. He could see so many ways this could go wrong, and he couldn't see any way it would go right. What the hell, if he was going to get into trouble, he'd make sure other people got into trouble as well.

"Sergeant, permission to speak with Lieutenant Hawkins. About duties here, Sergeant."

Sergeant Taylor was suspicious, but he couldn't think of a good reason to refuse. He watched Thomas like a hawk. Lieutenant Hawkins was covertly watching the four recruits, while talking at the table to one of the younger junior officers. Lieutenant Hawkins was doing most of the listening and very little of the talking.

"Sir," said Sergeant Taylor. "Rifleman Recruit O'Grady wishes to speak with you."

It was with some relief that Lieutenant Hawkins took his leave. "Duty calls, Nick. Carry on, O'Grady."

Thomas took a deep breath. "Sir, we've been able to lay our hands on some Sicilian whisky. Thought the Colonel might like to try some, Sir."

"Sicilian whisky? They don't make whisky in Sicily."

"Not officially, Sir."

Lieutenant Hawkins smelt something wrong. There was always one reliable way of dealing with that. "Mr Taylor, make sure that this whisky is drinkable."

Thomas waved Frank over, who produced a glass. Sergeant Taylor tasted it very cautiously. "Sicilian, you say, Rifleman Recruit O'Grady?"

"Yes, Sergeant."

Lieutenant Hawkins raised a questioning eyebrow.

"Tastes just like scotch, Sir."

"Not quite," said Thomas. He couldn't help himself. "A bit less peat, a bit more sunshine."

"And you would know that how, exactly, O'Grady?"

"My father, Sir." Thomas paused, and smiled inwardly at how much his father would hate this. "He was in the trade, Sir. Deliveries."

*****

The two Colonels and the Major-General relaxed in the most comfortable chairs in the Mess. Thomas and Frank approached, Frank carrying a tray with three glasses. The other Colonel was much younger than Colonel

Dalkeith, from a cavalry regiment. Thomas pushed aside the thought that he looked like a horse. The Major-General was about Colonel Dalkeith's age, thoughtful and quiet, and happy to let the two colonels snipe at each other with careful politeness.

"Ah, this is the fellow I was telling you about. Caught the fox that had been taking my peacocks. Caught it with his bare hands. Saw it myself." Colonel Dalkeith smiled indulgently.

"Remarkable," drawled the other Colonel. "Bit of a shame, really. It must have ruined a good hunt."

"It all depends," said the Major-General thoughtfully. "Fox hunting is a sport. The chase is the important part. It's the hunt that matters. Teaches equestrianism. The actual catching of the fox is secondary. Some of my best hunts have not caught a damned thing, but the rides were incredible. Catching a predator, that's different. Purpose is to catch the blighter, everything else is secondary. How did you do it, Rifleman?"

Thomas paused. Colonel Dalkeith gave a nod. "Man's shy, talking to officers. No need to worry, just answer honestly."

"Very good, Sir. Like I told you, Sir. I'm a Rifleman."

There was a silence. Finally, the Major-General broke the silence. "And?"

"That's it, Sir. Lieutenant Hawkins, Sir, he's taught us that Riflemen get the job done, whatever it takes. Sir."

Colonel Dalkeith and the Major-General laughed. The other Colonel looked annoyed. "I take it you save your best Mess silver for special occasions," he said, casually.

"Interesting whisky, this," interrupted the Major-General. "Didn't know they made whisky in Sicily."

"Not officially, Sir," said Lieutenant Hawkins, coming to Thomas' rescue.

"So, you've dragooned us into disposing of the contraband," said the Major-General. "Ha! The dragoon colonel has been dragooned."

The two colonels stopped looking at each other with contempt and shook their heads at the inane comment. Colonel Dalkeith looked thoughtfully at his whisky.

"Less peat. A much sharper taste than I would expect."

"Extra sunshine, Sir," said Lieutenant Hawkins.

"Not unpleasant. Not up to Highland standards," said the Major-General. "Better than the Irish heresies."

Thomas did his best to keep a straight face. The Major-General had been drinking an ordinary Scottish single malt.

"About this scavenger hunt, Garnet," the Major-General reminded Colonel Dalkeith. "Rifleman, another for each of us. Get the job done, whatever it takes. I like that. Is it true?"

Thomas desperately tried to look impassive.

"Of course it's true," said Colonel Dalkeith. The other Colonel just snorted.

"I'll arrange an exercise between your two regiments," the Major-General said cheerfully. "Now, about this scavenger hunt. What's the theme of the hunt, Garnet?"

"Cunning like a fox."

"Do you think that wise?" asked the other Colonel.

"I think it's a splendid chance for the officers to show initiative," said the Major-General. "Do whatever it takes. Wouldn't it be jolly if someone brought in a live fox, caught with their bare hands, eh Rifleman?"

*****

The car could carry four comfortably. There were five of them. In addition, Lady Dalkeith insisted on sitting in the back without being crowded. Peter was driving, because he was the only one who knew how to drive. Since Frank and young Windy were the smallest, they sat next to him, squashed on a single seat. That left Thomas to sit in the back with Lady Dalkeith, who was giving directions to Peter.

Thomas wasn't sure what sort of car it was. It was big and black and had leather seats and it bounced around more than a horse. At least with a horse, you could anticipate the jolts.

"Where are we going, Ma'am?" Thomas asked.

"To pay a visit to Teddie's regiment. Rifleman O'Grady. I know that you are not an honest man. Are you and your comrades resourceful looters?"

"Ma'am? I'm not sure I understand."

"Teddie was rude once too often about Garnet's regiment. Save the best silver for special occasions indeed. I will create a disturbance. You four rascals will remove their mess silver and we will drive off with it."

Thomas had so many questions he would have liked to ask. "Why us, Ma'am?"

"Because the regiment will be deployed to Persia shortly. I know that because Dickie can't keep a secret. The old hands in the Regiment are set in their ways. It's the new people who can be trained with the appropriate skills. That's what Garnet thinks. That's why he arranged for Lieutenant Hawkins to have the recruit platoon."

He'd got the answer to a question, and the answer just raised several other questions. He wasn't sure if he dared ask another question. "Appropriate skills, Ma'am?"

"Garnet believes that training for large set-piece battles when there is little likelihood of a large set-piece battle isn't a very productive use of time. The Regiment will be going to a place where there will be a lot of small-unit deployments. That means that these units will need to show initiative, because they won't always be able to ask for detailed instructions. That's what Garnet said."

Thomas wondered whether the Colonel said this before Lady Dalkeith had explained it to him. "Steal their Mess silver, Ma'am?" It seemed a safer question.

"Better that things go wrong here than in Persia. If things go wrong here, the worst that will happen is that you'll be flogged and confined to barracks. If things go wrong in Persia, it could be very unfortunate."

"How on Earth are we going to get their Mess silver, Ma'am?"

"That, Rifleman O'Grady, is something that you'll have to work out for yourselves. Initiative."

Thomas did not find this conversation reassuring. He decided to keep silent for the rest of the trip. They couldn't wander about in Riflemen uniforms. They'd be spotted straight away. Predators went hidden. That meant they needed dragoon uniforms. They'd also need to make sure that the owners of the uniforms didn't raise the alarm.

And the uniforms needed to fit, or else some sergeant would ask awkward questions. Just waylaying someone and taking their uniform wouldn't work. He also had the feeling that waylaying a dragoon might lead to problems. That meant they had to get into the QM stores. But first, they had to somehow find out what sort of disturbance Lady Dalkeith was arranging.

Since the car wouldn't drive itself, Peter had to stay with it. Frank, Windy and Thomas got out just before the gate. They needed to somehow stay hidden and being in the car wouldn't be a good start. While everyone's attention was on the car, the three of them tried to stay in the shadows near the guard room.

A guard room blocked the guard's view of things, and it provided some cover. Not much, but when the guards were not expecting anything and were just waiting to be relieved, it was enough.

Lady Dalkeith was not keeping her voice down. She told the Corporal of the Guard she needed to speak with the Officer of the Day. The Corporal quickly decided that the best course of action was to call the Duty Sergeant. The Duty Sergeant called the Duty Lieutenant. The Duty Lieutenant arrived, and by now there was a lot of noise and concern at the car, with no-one really knowing what was going on. The Duty Lieutenant called the Officer of the Day.

"What seems to be the problem, Lady Dalkeith?" he asked.

"It's a problem for you, Reggie. I thought I'd give you a warning that Dickie has decided to hold a snap inspection here first thing in the morning. Garnet put him up to it, and they hope to catch you out. You might want to get your people to make a start on getting the place into order."

"Why are you telling us, Lady Dalkeith?" The Officer of the Day was suspicious.

"I believe the term is payback. Garnet has taken his trollop into London once too often. He's as discrete as a crash of rhinoceri. Chop, chop, Reggie. Time's slipping by. Get your people moving. Now, I shall wait at the car and not get in your way. My driver needs to fix the engine. When he's done, we'll be off."

****

It was amazing. Dragoons were rushing about, too busy to pay any attention to anything other than what they were told to do. The camp was like an anthill that had been poked with a stick. Sergeants were shouting, junior officers were pointing, and dragoons were labouring. Thomas, Frank, and Windy watched as six troopers struggled to carry out an immensely heavy review stand from a store on to the parade ground. They got it there, and a sergeant told them to take it back to the store. Five minutes later, another six troopers were carrying it out again.

"We need to go to the stables," Thomas said. They had to find uniforms that fitted, and if he knew anything about the care of horses, it was that servants didn't wear their best clothes to do it in.

No-one paid much attention to them as they made their way towards the long building which had to be the stables. The smell of horse was unmistakeable. Keeping stables clean enough for an inspection was not going to be easy. The whitewashed brick walls had ingrained dirt that no amount of cleaning would remove.

Not that this stopped them trying. Half a dozen troopers were scrubbing away at the walls, and another dozen were brushing down the horses inside. As Thomas had thought, the troopers had hung their jackets on hooks on the stable wall, and everyone was concentrating on their work, trying to look as though they were working hard while doing as little as possible.

"You know, if we were enemy spies," said Windy, his voice trailing away.

"We are enemy spies," replied Peter. "We are here to steal Mess silver."

"Borrow," said Thomas.

"Property is theft; it's all looted stuff anyway," Peter replied.

Thomas ignored this. "We're going to need to keep our own jackets. When we leave, we'll need them. Slip a jacket over your own. Find one that fits."

There was a problem. There was only one jacket that fitted Windy. A sergeant's jacket.

"Who's going to believe that there could be a sergeant who isn't old enough to shave?" Windy said.

"Who ask a Sergeant?" Frank said with a shrug.

"Windy, try and look confident, assured. You're supposed to be a sergeant."

Something remarkable happened to Windy when he put the jacket on. He looked at the troopers cleaning the wall of the stable, and he shook his head sadly. The troopers noticed him noticing them, and they started working harder.

"Don't draw attention to yourself," whispered Thomas.

"Oh, dear me," said Windy, loudly. "It seems to me that some of you have mislaid your elbow grease. Trooper, what colour is this wall?"

"White, Sergeant."

"White, you say? Wrong. It's not white. It should be white, but it's not white. White is the colour of a wedding dress. Would a blushing bride want a dress the colour of that wall? I don't think so. I think you need to put your back into it, trooper, or I shall be very displeased. Do I make myself clear?"

"Yes, Sergeant."

Windy looked at Thomas and Frank. "As for you two, them horse brasses need to shine. Take them and get them shined. Don't forget to bring paint and brushes. Move."

"Why, Sergeant?" asked Thomas.

"Why, Sergeant?" mocked Windy. "What's the correct response when a sergeant tells you to do something? Good boys."

Thomas and Frank picked up trays with horse brass on and started to walk towards where they suspected the Officers' Mess was.

"Is that how we walk?" Windy said. "Slovenly and like a civilian? You was taught better than that. You can't march while carrying that, but you can walk in a soldier-like manner."

Frank muttered something under his breath, and Thomas suspected that it was not complimentary.

Thomas noticed an officer looking curiously at them, and then walking over. There was nowhere to hide.

"Sergeant, where are you taking those men?"

Thomas started to say something, but Windy spoke.

"Lieutenant said to make sure the brass was shining, Sir." It would have been more convincing if Windy's voice hadn't changed pitch half-way through and the Captain gave him a sharp glance.

"Which Lieutenant, Sergeant?" The Captain sounded on the verge of a temper tantrum. Red-faced, chubby cheeks, and impeccable uniform, tailored to fit perfectly on a slightly over-weight body.

"The new one, sir. Said we'd find good polish up by the Mess silver."

"The new Lieutenant? Lieutenant Carstairs? He's not in your chain of command, is he?"

"Not exactly, Sir. But the polish is there, Sir, and these men was cleaning them."

"And the paint?"

"Noticed that some of the stones by the Officers' Mess was looking a bit grey, Sir."

"And who gave you that instruction?"

"No-one, Sir. But word is that the inspection is going to be looking carefully at the Officers, Sir."

"What word is this, Sergeant?"

Don't get carried away, Thomas thought and prayed.

"Sergeant telegraph, Sir. Nothing official, just what we've heard. We've heard the Major-General has decided that if the officers aren't setting a good example, the men won't be properly led. He'd found some sloppiness when he'd inspected the 17th, and he's decided to crack down on officers. Deportment, awareness, that sort of thing. Word is that officially he's coming at 0700, but he'll actually arrive an hour early. That's the word among the Sergeants, Sir."

"Which regiment did Lieutenant Carstairs come from?" mused the Captain.

"The 17th, Sir."

"Sergeant, why aren't your boots regulation?"

"New regulations, Sir. It's on Standing Orders, Sir. Will that be all, Sir?"

"Carry on, Sergeant."

Thomas had seen which way the Captain had glanced when the Officers' Mess had been mentioned. He led the way, and then juddered to a halt as the Captain spoke to Windy.

"Aren't you a little young to be a Sergeant?"

"Gentleman-Ranker, Sir. Lieutenant said that class would out. Permission to carry on, Sir?"

The Captain nodded, and the three of them moved off as quickly as they could. They reached the Officers' Mess, which was now a hive of activity. Word had got around that the inspection would be looking at the officers and everyone seemed keen to make sure the Mess was spotless.

It wasn't spotless at the moment. It was chaos. Every piece of furniture had been piled up at end of the room, while troopers scrubbed the floor within an inch of its life. The Mess Corporal looked at them suspiciously.

"Everything's under control," he snapped. Tempers were getting short.

"Lieutenant Carstairs said that cleaning the room with the Mess silver in the room was a recipe for getting dirt on the silver. He sent us to move the silver to a place of safety."

"I haven't got the people to spare to move it."

"I've brought my own people. They'll carry it, clean it one last time. And, Corporal, you don't use that tone of voice."

One of the troopers cleaning the Mess room grinned at hearing the Corporal being told off.

Windy continued. "It seems that these men can work a lot harder. I'm not seeing the sweat on their brows. See to it, Corporal."

The troopers glared at the trooper who had unwisely grinned, and Windy indicated that Thomas and Frank should carry off the Mess silver.

None of it was easy to carry, and they had to make the pretence of trying to carry it without damaging it. Luckily, the punch bowl was enormous, and most of the plates and serving trays and cutlery fitted in it. They used cloths to stop it getting damaged.

"We'll be back for the rest," Windy said. "Put your backs into it," he snapped as Thomas and Frank staggered under the weight.

Out across the parade ground.

"Sergeant, where are you going with that?" It was the busy-body Captain.

"Moisture, Sir," said Windy. "The silver has got moisture beneath the surface. It needs a good airing if they're to shine properly, Sir."

"Of course. Carry on, Sergeant."

"I have thought," said Frank. "How we all fit in car with Mess silver?"

Thomas thought. "Peter drives the car with the Colonel's Lady and the silver. We walk."

"I have better idea." Frank pointed to a motorcycle with sidecar near the gate.

"None of us know how to drive it," said Windy.

"How hard can it be?" asked Thomas. "I think I know the basics."

Five minutes later, they'd hastily thrown the Mess silver into the car, and Peter drove off with it and Lady Dalkeith.

Five minutes after that, Thomas had worked out how to start the motorcycle, and drove unsteadily off out of the gate. They'd not got far, when Windy shouted at him to stop.

"I don't know how."

Perhaps fortunately, in answering, Thomas had turned in his seat, and lost his balance, and the motorbike fell over and into a ditch.

"That's how," Thomas said. "Why do you want to stop?"

"Paint a slogan on the wall. So that they think someone else is responsible."

The motorbike was unsalvageable, so they walked back anyway. They left the dragoon jackets, and on the wall was a slogan. They weren't sure if the Colonel's Lady would approve or not.

"Votes for Women."

*****

The guests at the Mess dinner returned from their scavenger hunt.

"Teddie," asked Lady Dalkeith. "I drove past your barracks, and it seemed to be in a bit of turmoil. No problems, I hope."

"Turmoil?"

"All sorts of activity and shouting and people rushing around. It seemed a strange time for it."

"It keeps people on their toes," Colonel de Villiers said, unconvincingly. "I had better go and check on how they're getting on." He got up and signalled for his driver.

When Colonel de Villiers had left, Major-General Younghusband snorted. "If I'm not much mistaken, Maeve, Teddie was caught by surprise by your news."

"Possibly, Dickie. It might be quite jolly to inspect them first thing, don't you think? See what it was all about."

"If I didn't know better, I would suspect you of scheming and manipulation, Maeve. Garnet, this scavenger hunt. I'm looking forward to seeing what people have come up with. Let's have a look, shall we? I expect you want me to be the impartial judge."

Everyone dutifully rose and headed outside. A suggestion from the Major-General wasn't a Royal Command, but it wasn't far off. The first thing everyone noticed was a bull being held by three rather worried looking riflemen. A fourth rifleman was ready with bucket and spade. Lieutenant Hawkins stepped forward, and the bull seemed to glare at him. The bull was not getting any calmer.

"Lieutenant Hawkins," said Colonel Dalkeith mildly. "Care to explain. Quickly, so we can return it."

"It's a bull, Colonel."

"Remarkable piece of observation, Lieutenant. I can see that it's a bull. Perhaps a bit more of an explanation."

"This is the First Battalion of the Rifle Brigade. On the range, we always hit the bull."

"And the eyepatch?"

"The bull's eye, Colonel."

The Major-General chuckled. "You seem to have taught your officers and men to have a pride in the Regiment, Garnet."

Colonel Dalkeith indicated with a wave of his hand that the bull should be removed from the camp. "Return him to his owner. I don't want to see beef on the menu tomorrow." They turned their attention to a young Lieutenant.

"Lieutenant Furley-Smith, why are you dressed as a woman?"

"Fox furs, Colonel. I'm cunning and I'm dressed like a fox."

"Technically, you're like a vixen."

"Do you see dressing up as a woman as a useful skill for a soldier, Lieutenant?" Major-General Younghusband sounded curious.

"Yes, Sir. When on deployment far from home, it's likely Mess Dinners will have a gender imbalance, Sir. Helps with dance partners."

"Let's see what you've brought to the party, Maeve."

Lady Dalkeith nodded to Peter, who was standing by the boot of her car. He opened it, and stepped aside, rather hoping he would not be noticed. Everyone moved closer, and there was a lengthy silence, punctuated by a few coughs.

"Additions to the Mess silver," she said, seemingly not noticing the silence. "Teddie suggested it needed sprucing up."

"It will be returned, won't it, Colonel."

"Absolutely, Sir. We'll hand it over to the rightful owner. I shall personally hand it over to the rightful owner just as soon as he makes himself known to me."

"Dishonestly acquired, Garnet," admonished the Major-General.

"With respect, Dickie," said Lady Dalkeith, "it's been acquired in exactly the way Mess silver is usually acquired. The punch bowl was acquired during the First

Sikh War, Spoils of War. Teddie took great pleasure in explaining this to me."

"But you're not at war with Teddie's dragoons," Major-General Younghusband said, suspecting that he was losing the argument.

"On the contrary," said Colonel Dalkeith. "You said that you would arrange an exercise between the regiments. That means we operate as though we were at war."

"But the war, the exercise, dammit, hasn't started yet."

"The Royal Navy boasts of Copenhagening the enemy fleet, attacking before the enemy were ready. If the Navy can do it, so can we. Besides, they should have taken better care of their silver. Sloppy guards are inexcusable, peacetime or wartime."

Major-General Younghusband thought carefully how to phrase this. "I think I see why this regiment has a reputation of being full of rogues and scoundrels. God help the merchants of Persia."

Thomas, Windy, and Frank returned from their walk back. They'd had to dive out of the way of a car that was being driven at a reckless speed, and the ditch they'd dived into had been muddy. Their uniforms were a mess. Their dress uniforms.

"Sergeant Taylor's going to be livid," said Windy.

It looked like Windy's prediction was about to be proven correct. Sergeant Taylor was heading in their direction. He was just about to say something, when Lady Dalkeith had a quick word with Lieutenant Hawkins, who then came over.

"Line of duty, Sergeant. They assisted me in getting the bull. I'm confident they'll be presentable in time for morning roll call."

Sergeant Taylor wasn't happy about this, but he had no choice. "I'll be paying very close attention to you at roll call."

"Carry on, Sergeant." Once Sergeant Taylor left, Lieutenant Hawkins looked at the three bedraggled recruits.

"Lady Dalkeith said that you'd performed a service for her. Despite what you might think, she's not in the Chain of Command. She doesn't give you orders. Is that understood?"

"Yes, Sir."

Windy was unwise enough to add to this. "Sir, it's just that Lady Dalkeith is, well, she kind of says things, and you just do what she says."

"Now you know better."

"Lieutenant Hawkins, I'd like a word with these three soldiers, if you don't mind." Lady Dalkeith had approached quietly.

"Of course, Lady Dalkeith." With that, Lieutenant Hawkins returned to the Mess dinner.

"You four needn't look so smug. I made a request of Lieutenant Hawkins, which he graciously granted. That's different from giving orders. He's quite correct. I'm not in the chain of command, so you'd do well to remember that. I wanted to thank you for your assistance. The outcome was satisfactory. I trust you learned from the exercise."

The four soldiers nodded.

"What, exactly, have you learned? O'Grady?"

"That guards are not useful if they don't do their job, and that once you've got past the guards, people see what they expect to see, because the guards keep out outsiders, even if they don't."

"Barry?"

"That you don't need to hide to hide. And that is easy to hide in confusion."

"Grant?"

"That despite what sergeants seem to think, it's not possible to repair a car engine and keep a uniform clean."

"Miller?"

"I like being a sergeant. It felt like it fitted, kind of."

"Yes, I rather think you might be one of nature's sergeants. But you need to learn to walk before you try running."

"Ma'am, can I ask a question?" asked Thomas.

"You can ask."

"It's, well, that business about what you said about the Colonel and London. It's not true, is it?"

Lady Dalkeith raised an eyebrow. "That's a rather impertinent question. All I will say is that it is both true and very misleading. It may be unfashionable, but Garnet and I have been happily married for over 35 years. One other lesson you should have learned from tonight. The regiment is like a family. We may squabble among ourselves, but we're unified against all outsiders. You had best get back to your duties. I rather suspect that you might want to get cleaned up."

As the soldiers left, Lady Dalkeith put her hand into her bag, and touched an old, much-read book, and she smiled as she remembered a time in Boston nearly forty years ago. She'd been a young woman then, and bored beyond measure with the expectations of Society, with no prospect of anything approaching excitement. And there had been an English Army officer, who had seen her reading a book at the harbour.

He'd noticed what book it was, and they had got into an argument about it. He'd invited her to continue the discussion over tea, and then he'd added: "Provided you don't throw it in the sea, which I gather is how tea is made here."

He'd said it with such a straight face. Over tea, he'd told of the life of an Army officer, the places he'd been to, and the places he might go to. She'd thought about what life held for her here; wooed by spineless young men who agreed with everything she said in the hopes of winning her favour, marrying a suitable husband, doing the rounds of Society, talking to the same people year after year, and quite possibly never setting foot outside Boston.

They'd married within the year, which scandalised both Boston and his regiment. He had to leave his regiment, and he'd joined the Rifles, and been with it ever since, and they'd seen many places in the world. She had been extraordinarily fortunate, and all because of a book.

They each carried a copy of the book wherever they went. The Domestic Manners of the Americans, by Fanny Trollope.

*****

The Colonel explained things to Lieutenant Hawkins. It had made sense then. It made less sense now, out here in the field. He'd explained that the recruits of his platoon were not yet familiar with operating as part of the battalion and trying to do so in the field would be a recipe for confusion. But the Colonel had also said that the exercise would be good experience for the recruits and that they were far enough advanced in their training to contribute.

The Colonel had gone on to explain that the recruit platoon would operate independently. The dragoons had been tasked with finding a weakness in the defence line the Rifles held, and then exploiting it. That was their function.

The Rifles were tasked with holding the line, ten miles from Tenant Hill to the river.

"Colonel de Villiers will push the boundaries of the letter of the restrictions. He'll know that a battalion trying to hold a ten-mile line will be spread thin. For the purpose of this exercise, his casualties will return to their base of operations, and they can then return as reinforcements. In effect, he has an infinite supply of troops, but he can only use a regiment at a time. Our casualties stay casualties. I'm giving you a free hand, Hawkins. See if your ideas work in the field." The Colonel smiled. "They have to return to their base of operations. I want you and your men to stop them being able to return. No base, no reinforcements. Are your men ready for it?"

"No. But we'll get the job done, somehow."

That was then. Now, with just himself, Sergeant Taylor, five corporals, and thirty-two Riflemen recruits, he wasn't so confident.

And Major Brampton, he added. Major Brampton was on Major-General Younghusband's staff, and he was acting as an umpire. Young, ambitious, getting all the right connections so he could get the appropriate promotions, and he hadn't been in the field for several years. He was already puffing heavily, panting and struggling to keep up, even though the men were in full kit and he was only carrying a clipboard.

"You've made your point, Lieutenant. This is an unsustainable speed."

"Major, we're sustaining the pace. This is Rifle Brigade pace."

"Regulations say that this pace is not sustainable for more than twenty minutes. We've been going for an hour. The men need a rest." Major Brampton was struggling. The men were walking along in a line of twos, familiar with these cross-country marches and looking to be in no distress.

"Except as operational conditions might demand otherwise," Lieutenant Hawkins said. "The enemy are not going to wait for us, so operational conditions apply."

*****

"What he say?" Frank asked Thomas. They were heading across fields towards a wood on a small rise.

"That we can't walk this fast."

"So, what are we doing?"

Thomas shrugged. "Breaking Army regulations, I think. Again." He was surprised how much of being a good soldier seemed to involve breaking regulations.

The ground was muddy. Very muddy. Maybe some sort of river flood plain, Thomas wondered, trying to remember his lessons at school. Definitely heavy going for horses. From a distance, it had looked like it was easy going, but looks were deceiving. Unless you checked the ground out, you'd naturally take this route.

The going got easier once they started walking up the slight hill to the wood.

"Why we not with regiment?" Frank asked.

"Because the rest of the regiment don't like us."

"And why we leave so early?"

Thomas shrugged. "No-one asked me for my opinion."

The four were still grumbling when they reached the woods, not long before dawn.

"Why was there all the hurry?" Windy asked, as they were allowed to fall out in the woods. "We set out during the night, march flat out to get here, and now that we're here, they tell us to sit around and wait."

"That's the Army," said Peter with a shrug. "Hurry up and wait. Always been that way, always will be. Ain't no reason for it."

"Gather round," said Lieutenant Hawkins. "Some of you are probably wondering why we had to get here before sunrise, and then wait. The reason is that the exercise starts at sunrise, and we're now in position. With luck, the enemy won't know we're here."

"Sir, does that mean that we started the exercise before the exercise started?" Thomas couldn't help himself. He knew he would get into trouble for asking the question, but his curiosity got the better of him.

"Nonsense," said Lieutenant Hawkins. "We haven't yet started the exercise. You're still in training, and this is a training night march in full kit."

Major Brampton had already objected and found that the rules simply said that the exercise started when it started, and there was nothing that specified that the troops had to be in barracks at the start time. He was starting to hate the Rifles, this platoon in particular, and especially the trouble-making Lieutenant Hawkins.

Lieutenant Hawkins explained what was going on to the men. Sergeant Taylor was stony-faced. "Our job is not to stop the enemy going out. It's to stop them going back to base."

"Lieutenant," said Major Brampton. "It might be a good idea if you didn't keep referring to your opponents as the enemy. This is an exercise. It's not actual war."

"Thank you, Major Brampton. When I've finished explaining, one squad at a time will move carefully to the edge of the wood and get a good look at the lie of the land. In particular, look carefully at the base of operations of the enemy. This will be regarded as a farmhouse, although it will actually just be a collection of tents. Nonetheless, these tents are to be treated like a farm house. Remember that this is training for a war, so don't go thinking it's just an exercise. If you do that, you'll go into the real thing with bad habits, and then you'll get shovelled under. All clear so far?"

There were wary nods. The soldiers weren't sure about this. This was sounding suspiciously like they might be required to think. Thomas wondered how much trouble Lieutenant Hawkins was going to get into.

Lieutenant Hawkins continued. "Then, when every squad is familiar with the lay of the land, the platoon will break into sections. I'll be with section 1, Sergeant Taylor with section 2, Corporal Ross with section 3, and Major Brampton with section 4."

"I must again protest. I am an umpire and an observer, not a participant."

"And you will be observing and not participating with section 4. Corporal Barrett, remember that Major Brampton is an observer, and not in the chain of command, and is not able to give you orders. One Section will go around to the far side of the farmhouse. Two Section to the left, Three Section to the right, and Four Section will stay here.

"Lieutenant Hawkins. Do I understand correctly? You're breaking the platoon down into four sections that will be operating independently? That's not possible. Regulations clearly state that the smallest unit for independent action in the field is the platoon."

"Major Brampton, while I appreciate your concerns with how I run my platoon, and your long experience in conducting operations in the field, that's not what's happening." Lieutenant Hawkins' voice had taken on an edge and Thomas understood why he was still just a Lieutenant.

"Now. Once in position, each squad in the section will operate independently of each other. We shall have eight independently operating squads. Four men with an officer or an NCO. The Army doesn't think it's possible, but we're Rifles, so we do the impossible. This has been approved by Colonel Dalkeith. Because you'll be operating independently, I'm going to explain exactly what you're going to do. When the exercise starts, the enemy will follow procedure. One squadron will go out to probe for weak spots in the defence line. They're not our target. A second squadron will go out to act as close support, so they'll have fresh horses to exploit any weakness straight away, before it can get plugged.

They're not our target. We let them go. They'll leave one squadron to guard the base. They're our target. Any questions so far?"

Windy hesitantly spoke. "Sir, 200 troopers in a squadron. There's 32 rifles in a platoon."

"That's right. We outnumber them."

"I don't understand, Sir."

"They know regulations as well as we do. As Major Brampton has kindly explained, regulations say that the smallest operating unit is the platoon. When they come under attack from eight different directions, they'll know they're facing a minimum of eight platoons, 250 rifles. Our rifles outrange theirs, so they have to close with us. They've got speed and mobility, so they'll try to take each unit one at a time. Whichever squad they head for will fight a holding action, with the support of the other squad in that section. Once the enemy have been committed to the action, the other six squads will advance, take the base, burn it to the ground, eliminate the enemy staff, and prepare to receive attack. The squadron will hear the commotion and return to base to deal with us. Open ground in heavy going against riflemen in cover? They'll come charging in, using speed to take us by surprise. That is what doctrine says they will do. They'll be disorganised, confused, unprepared and with endless courage. We will massacre them."

"I must again protest, Lieutenant Hawkins. Your plan is unworkable. What is more, it breaks with regulations."

Lieutenant Hawkins drew a deep breath before answering. "Major Brampton. I command this platoon. You are, as you have said many times, merely an observer. I have used tactics like this in action, where real bullets were used, and I lived to tell the tale. Granted that the Army does not seem to have seen fit to listen to the tale, but that's another matter. Your protest is noted, and by the end of the day, we'll have a clearer idea about the effectiveness of my ideas, or whether your experience of combat from the position of a staff desk outweighs mine. Colonel Dalkeith instructed me to test out my irregular ideas. He wonders if irregular warfare calls for irregular tactics. He has given me clear instructions, Sir, to test my ideas out, and I intend to carry out the orders given to me by my Colonel. So, Sir, I will respectfully ask you to observe, as that is your role, and not to interfere with how I run my platoon."

"You know," Peter muttered under his breath, "I can see why he's only a Lieutenant."

*****

The four soldiers watched and waited. Being on their own was unusual. Corporal Robson and the first squad were at the other end of the wood, out of sight. Close enough that they could provide supporting fire to each other, but out of sight. They could easily imagine that they were alone, that it was just the four of them.

And Major Brampton.

"You got everything you need, Sir?" asked Windy. "Enough water?"

Major Brampton said nothing.

"If you need anything, ask. We probably haven't got it, but if you don't ask, you don't get, as they say."

Major Brampton sighed. "Soldier, I'm only going to say this once. I don't talk to anyone below the rank of sergeant."

"Fine by us," muttered Peter, loudly enough to be heard, and quietly enough to be ignored.

"What did you say, soldier?"

"Fine day for us, Sir," Thomas said quickly. "It's going to be a clear, fine day."

Ten minutes later, it started to rain.

"That's your fault," Peter said to Thomas.

They creeped cautiously to the edge of the wood to get a better idea of the lay of the land.

The wood was on a slight rise. Not enough of a rise to be called a hill, but just enough to be a bit drier than the farm land. At least, Thomas assumed that it was farm land. Fields interrupted by hedges, and with a winding, fast-moving stream cutting diagonally across the fields. The stream was full to the top of the bank. A rather dilapidated building stood next to the stream, about three hundred yards away from them. The building had a water wheel that was busily turning and was next to a small bridge that spanned the stream. About half a mile beyond the building was a collection of tents, with hundreds of horses being exercises in the vicinity.

"That bridge is key," said Frank.

"For us. Not for them. They can jump the stream. We can't." Thomas was confident about this.

"You know," Peter said. "if we just walk off, there is nothing to stop us. Maybe there will be jobs in the village, maybe a station nearby, we could go to London."

"That would be desertion," whispered Windy. "They hang you for that."

"That's not true. They hang you for getting caught. There is no-one to stop us."

"There's the Major."

Frank interrupted. "If he get in way, he have throat smile." He paused. "It joke. Time to desert is when we have loot. No good to desert when poor."

Thomas decided not to mention how much the rifle was worth. "Movement at the camp," he said.

*****

Squadron 1 had been sent out to probe for weak spots. They'd been given their orders, to test up and down the line, to avoid contact, and to keep the defensive line busy. Cavalry could move faster than infantry, and for longer. Infantry had the advantage of firepower at a point; cavalry had the advantage of being able to cover more points. The job of Squadron 1 was to keep the infantry constantly having to keep moving position, to wear them out and overload their staff.

Colonel de Villiers had sent Squadron 2 to act as close support, with orders to exploit any weak spots that might be found. Squadron 1 would fire off flares every so often. Red flares for stop, green flares for go. The infantry would get used to seeing flares, and this was the quickest and simplest way to get information between the squadrons.

Staff work would be so much easier with instant communication to units in the front. Telephone lines were possible in long-term defence positions, but not practical for advancing cavalry. It was always difficult once things started. You gave your orders. You then had to wait and see what happened. Reports would come in, but often long after the event, and things changed with bewildering speed in the field. You had to stay calm, and the most important lesson you had to learn was to avoid constant changes of a plan at every little thing. Constant changes could reduce a well-trained regiment into a confused mob, a rabble.

Most messages had to be physically carried, and cavalry could move faster than infantry. That was why Squadron 1 had to keep probing and testing, to overload Dalkeith's staff with conflicting information.

He kept Squadron 3 in reserve, guarding the base and ready to move up at the critical moment. He had explained to them that guarding the base was not a passive role. Infantry, with their greater fire density and their lack of mobility could hunker down and sit tight. Cavalry had to send out constant patrols, check the ground, and disrupt the enemy before they got close. Space was the friend of the cavalry.

Squadron 2 left the base, and Squadron 3 started sending out small 10-trooper patrols on a rolling coverage of the area up to half a mile from the camp.

*****

Colonel Dalkeith didn't like having his staff base on the hill. It enabled him to see, more or less, the whole line, but it was right on the flank, and the other flank was over ten miles away. Getting orders out there would be time-consuming. He worried that he'd be able to see what was happening, but that he would be unable to do anything about it.

With such a long line to defend, and so few troops to do it, he couldn't afford to have troops tied down. He'd deployed as best he could, with well-advanced pickets to give as much warning as possible. De Villiers would send probes to try and draw his men into one place, to draw them out of position.

Pickets covering the likely lines of approach and forcing scouting patrols to make detours. Leave a few apparent holes to draw in their main force into a killing ground.

Then there was the wild card of Hawkins' platoon. When Hawkins explained his ideas, they sounded plausible. The trouble was, ideas often sounded plausible until you tried to put them into practise. The reports said that Hawkins had tried them out in the field, with mixed success.

Hawkins said that this was because no-one let him try out his ideas properly. His point was that very small, interlocking units, squad-sized, would overload any enemy staff work, and in irregular situations, could take on irregular forces without being constrained by regimental structures.

His commanders said that his ideas were impractical, as they relied on junior NCOs acting with a level of intelligence and initiative that they couldn't possibly have.

Warfare was changing. He could see that. What he couldn't see was exactly what those changes were going to be. He'd never rise beyond Colonel, so this regiment was the focus of his attention. They would be deployed to Persia soon, and they had to be ready for that.

He sighed. One thing that would change things would be the ability to talk to his commanders close to the action. So many methods had been tried; heliograph, flags, telephone lines, and not one of them was without major faults.

*****

Well, Lieutenant Hawkins had been right so far Thomas thought, as he watched the second squadron of riders leaving the base. He'd said that the third squadron would remain at the base to guard it, and that was what they had to deal with.

Once the two departing squadrons had gone far away, their instructions were to try and work their way closer to the enemy base.

"If you're seen, if they come after you, get clear and go to ground. They haven't got the manpower to block attacks from eight different directions, so it's important to keep the threats from each direction, so don't get caught. They can move faster than you can, so don't try to outrun them. Hide, ambush, or just use your rifles and blow them away. Whatever you think will work. Regulations say that you're not clever enough to do this, that you can't do your job without someone telling you exactly what to do every step of the way. I've told Colonel Dalkeith that you can. Don't let me down." That had been what Lieutenant Hawkins had said.

They had started to move once the second squadron was out of sight. They'd wondered about heading for the bridge and the building, but Thomas shook his head.

"Too obvious. They'll be watching it. We don't want to get spotted."

"How are we going to get across the stream?" Windy asked.

"How deep's the stream?" Peter asked. "Given how fast its flowing, it can't be very deep."

"There's no way of telling," said Windy. "I can't swim."

"If it's not deep, you won't need to. If we can get a good look at that water wheel, we'll get a good idea how deep the water is."

Thomas thought for a moment. "We can't cross at the bridge, but if we can get to the building, we can see whether or not we can cross anywhere."

"We'll need to get there unseen." Windy sounded doubtful.

"Long grass, mud, shouldn't be a problem."

That was when they came up against their first problem. They needed to use cover to get there, which involved crawling in places to remain unseen. Major Brampton was a problem.

"I am an observer, a neutral. I have no intention of crawling in the mud."

"But Sir, they'll see you."

"That's not my problem. I'm an umpire. People are *supposed* to see me."

"You'll be giving away our position, Sir."

"That's really not my problem."

Frank started to put his hand to his knife, and Thomas put a hand on his arm to stop him. Frank thought. "You right. People know he with us. They ask us where he is."

Out of the corner of his eye, Thomas saw Peter taking some paper out of his pack. It looked like paper from the Major's clipboard. Peter nodded, then dropped the papers on the ground behind Major Brampton. The wind caught them and started to blow them around.

"Sir," said Thomas, pointing.

"My papers. Grab them."

The four riflemen didn't move. "Can't, Sir. You're not in our Chain of Command. Regulations say we can't take orders from you, Sir."

"I'm ordering you to get them," he shouted, starting to rush around to collect them. As he did so, the riflemen dropped to the ground, out of sight, and moved off as best they could manage.

Once Major Brampton had caught his papers, the riflemen had disappeared from sight. He shook his head at their stupidity. He might not know where they are, but he knew where they were going. To see the water wheel on the building. He started walking in that direction.

After a few moments, the riflemen started to follow the Major, staying out of sight in the long grass. It would have been harder if he had been looking around. As it was, he just walked straight towards the building.

*****

As Colonel de Villiers had expected, the reports coming back were confusing. The probes at the front were running into opposition earlier than had been estimated, but Dalkeith couldn't have his main line that far forward. That meant he'd pushed his pickets a long way forward. That meant that concentration at one point could punch a hole through the pickets, then they could get behind the rest of the pickets, cut them off, and blind the Rifles.

It wasn't yet time to commit Squadron 3. He'd just send a message to Squadron 1 to focus their efforts.

Squadron 3 weren't fully ready to be fully trusted. Reports were coming in from their patrols, and some of these were confused. They'd reported that the ground conditions were awful by the stream. That was straightforward enough and only to be expected. Heavy rain, low-lying ground, river flow, bound to be heavy going. It would be a surprise if it was anything else. The Squadron was marking the worst of the areas.

Some of the patrols were showing poor fire discipline, shooting at shadows. Simple arithmetic told him that. They were too far from the Rifles' front for them to be here. Not enough time for them to have got here, and any unit that had got out here would be isolated from any possible support. There were too many reports too widely separated to be plausible. Just shadows. This was what good staff work was about, evaluating the reliability of reports. However, he wasn't going to take chances. Just in case, he instructed a couple of patrols to look into these shadows.

Of course, Lieutenant Campbell had managed to get his patrol lost. He had interesting ideas, and he was very keen, but quite hopeless in the field. Go to the building. Check out the bridge and the building. Place the bridge under observation and be ready to surprise infantry trying to cross the bridge with his damn fool idea. How hard could that be? And not one report coming back.

It was tempting to send another patrol to find him, but he was already getting thin, and needed to keep his forces ready for the main event, not use them in little packets here and there.

*****

Colonel Dalkeith was getting reports back from the pickets. There had been a lot of activity all along that line. Constant probes, nothing pressed home, and then quiet. It was clear that there would soon be a strong probe in one place. He wanted to pull the pickets back in so that the probe would meet thin air.

But that would require rapid communication. By the time the orders had reached the pickets, it would be too late. The officers out on the picket line knew that their job was to disrupt and delay, not to try and stop, that they were to pull back if they were being hard pressed.

It was odd how much initiative junior officers were required to show, and yet how little support they were given when they did so. There were senior officers who took action against junior officers who made a mistake, which led to the junior officers doing everything by Regulations, so if anything did go wrong, they had a ready-made excuse.

He'd been Colonel of the Battalion for some time now. Fifteen years, and he'd go no higher. He still couldn't get the balance between encouraging initiative and punishing stupid mistakes.

He'd told the pickets to keep an eye on those on each flank, and to pull back if they did. Better they pull back a bit too soon than stay and get isolated.

As for what Lieutenant Hawkins was getting up to, that was another matter. There was nothing that could be done to help. His platoon was on its own. That was the point of this, but it was a worry. He had no way of knowing what was happening there.

Something had to be done to resolve this communication problem. That was for the future. He looked carefully at what he could see in the here and now.

"Take a message to Captain Filleul of B Company. The pickets in front of him are pulling back. I expect the dragoons will try and exploit the hole fairly soon and I expect his company to get them in the kill zone."

Colonel Dalkeith measured the distances with his eye. It would be touch and go if the message arrived in time.

*****

They hadn't expected this. Lieutenant Hawkins had said that the dragoons left would be guarding the base, but half a dozen small groups of riders came out and were circling the base. They didn't seem to be in any great hurry. They stopped every so often to hammer in a stake.

"Ranging marks," Peter told Thomas.

One group of six riders – five troopers and a junior officer – made straight for the bridge. They got to within fifty yards of the stream, and then stopped. They dismounted, and the officer walked forward a few steps, obviously testing the ground. He returned to his men, spoke to one of them, who mounted up and rode back towards the base.

Then the dragoons saw Major Brampton on the other side of the stream from them. They walked their horses to the bridge, looking around as though they suspected some sort of trap. Two of the horses were struggling in the mud and seemed to be carrying a heavy load.

*****

That was unexpected, thought Thomas. The cavalry patrol had seen Major Brampton, had approached him, had dismounted because of the slippery mud, hadn't seen the riflemen until it was too late. That wasn't what Thomas thought was unusual.

Major Brampton and the officer of the small cavalry patrol, Lieutenant Campbell, were arguing. They were arguing about the number of casualties the troopers would have taken when the riflemen opened fire on them. That wasn't the unexpected part.

What was unexpected was that Major Brampton had ruled that the troopers would have taken one casualty before getting out of range.

"With all due respect, Major" said Lieutenant Campbell, "I'm not convinced. There's no cover, we were dismounted and either had to mount and have our horses struggle through the mud or try and run. On foot we would have to cross the bridge, and on horse we would be highly visible targets. Not one of us would have made it." Lieutenant Campbell spoke with quiet, calm assurance, the voice of a man who was supremely self-confident.

"They're only recruits," said Major Brampton. "They would have shot wildly."

"Major Brampton, if they're only recruits, then they're damned good recruits. In all conscience, I'm assuming we were wiped out, and returning to base on that basis."

"Lieutenant Campbell, I've made a ruling."

"And Colonel de Villiers said that we had to take the exercise seriously. Come here, Rifleman."

Thomas could see that he didn't have much choice in the matter.

"That was neat work, Rifleman. Where's your officer?"

"No idea, Sir."

"He must be here somewhere."

It took a while to explain, and Thomas got the impression that Lieutenant Campbell wasn't entirely convinced.

"Permission to speak, Sir."

"Go ahead, Rifleman."

"I've been thinking, Sir."

"I'm sure your sergeant has warned you about that, but do go on."

"If your patrol has been wiped out, Sir, when you return to base, it's as reinforcements, isn't it, Sir? Does that mean that as reinforcements, you wouldn't know what happened here?"

"That would be a logical conclusion to draw. There would also be a delay, so I'll give my men a half hour break before heading back to give no report because new reinforcements can't give reports on things they've not been involved with."

Out of the corner of his eye, Thomas saw that Peter was putting something into his pack. Must he steal *everything* that wasn't tied down?

"Um, Sir, the stuff on those two horses?" He had to distract the Lieutenant somehow.

"Well spotted, Rifleman. You see, Major. Damned good recruit. It's a little scheme of mine. It's a machine gun. Dragoons have mobility but not firepower. This changes that. We can move around, find a good spot. Combine firepower and mobility. Of course, it would work better if we were able to get it off the horses and assembled, but the theory is still sound."

"Yes, Sir." Thomas had learned that you never went far wrong saying that.

"Carry on, Rifleman." Lieutenant Campbell and Major Brampton continued their discussion.

Thomas wanted to listen to the discussion. It was obviously an urbane and civil row, and he was enjoying seeing Major Brampton getting more and more annoyed. But they had to work out what to do next and slipping off while Major Brampton was arguing seemed like the best option.

*****

One thing was obvious, thought Colonel Dalkeith, and that was that Teddie was making use of flares to pass basic information. There was an easy enough counter to this. He just needed to have flare guns distributed to his own people, and totally confuse that set of information flow.

That was the trouble. It was easy enough to mess up the information flow, but it was not so easy to have a rapid, reliable, and accurate flow of information for your own use. Battlefields had become larger and more complicated than in the past. Wellington had a line that was about two miles long at Waterloo. A message could reach any part of the line within ten minutes. When the regiment was deployed to Persia, parts of his command could easily be fifty miles away, and the communication systems were essentially the same.

His father had always told him that if troops had been properly trained, they could be trusted. "It's not the Generals who know what your troops can and can't do. It's the Sergeants."

Of course, trusting the men didn't actually mean trusting them. They were still rogues and scoundrels. They were poorly paid, and the pay was often delayed, especially when on deployment. Inevitably, the men would find ways around this, and civilians often didn't like this. His men were no angels, nor were they the blackguards they were often portrayed as.

He allowed himself a private smile. He'd done well. Command of a regiment, a wife he loved, and a son just finishing at Oxford who would have the advantage of being the son of a Colonel, rather than the son of a Sergeant, as he had been.

He could hear his wife outside, making sure that the messengers were fed and had water, and that their equipment was acceptable. She shouldn't be there, but it was difficult to stop her going where she wanted to go. Talking to the officers and men and fussing over them. Not for the first time, he thought that if she had been a man, she'd have made a remarkable RSM.

Time to stop wool-gathering. He had no idea what Lieutenant Hawkins was up to, there was nothing he could do, and this would quite probably be something he'd have to get used to when they went to Persia.

"Sir, compliments of Lieutenant Furley-Smith. He wants clarification on the rules, Sir. He's taken a dragoon patrol prisoner. He said that the rules say that he has to release the dragoons so they can return as reinforcements, Sir. However, he said that the rules say nothing about the horses, and that as spoils of war, they might be considered to have fallen into our hands, and therefore not to be released. He's holding them until he gets your clarification on the rules, Sir."

Colonel Dalkeith shook his head in amusement. Regardless of what the decision was, those dragoons had been taken out of action for several hours. "Major-General? Do you have a ruling?"

"Your chaps are very devious and conniving rascals, Colonel. Dragoons without horses are no challenge, and an exercise is supposed to be a challenge. Let's not make things too easy for you."

Colonel Dalkeith acknowledged this and passed the message on. He was confident that shortly later, he'd be asked for a ruling about saddles and equipment. A messenger burst into the tent, panting and red with exertion. "Sir, compliments of Captain Hopkins," he panted. "Explosions on his front. Rather a lot of them. He said that his Umpire told him that he was coming under artillery fire. He's digging in, but asks for orders, Sir."

Major-General Younghusband chuckled. "Oh yes, Colonel. A little wrinkle in the exercise. Colonel de Villiers has just received pre-planned artillery support. Just buried charges, but it's simulating artillery."

Colonel Dalkeith hurried to the map, studied it briefly, and then started issuing orders. When the artillery lifted, they'd probe there and make a push. If he could get his troops back a bit, he could turn that area into a kill zone. Getting them back in time was going to be tough.

*****

Colonel de Villiers frowned. "Say that again?"

"Sir, Squadron 1 reports explosions along the central probe line. They've no idea what's causing them. They can't probe while they're going on. They request orders, Sir."

Major-General Younghusband's ADC coughed. "Ah, Colonel de Villiers. It's at this point that I'm instructed to tell you that it seems that Colonel Dalkeith has artillery supporting him. Major-General Younghusband expects you to deal with a changing situation in an appropriate manner."

Colonel de Villers tried to remain calm as he studied the map. "Dug-in infantry with artillery support. I see Major-General de Villiers has confidence in our ability to rise to a challenge. Squadron 1 is to make a show in front centre. Look big. Lots of movement and show. They're to stay out of range, but keep probing, and keep the riflemen watching them. Squadron 2 is to make a wide approach. Very wide. This route." He pointed on the map.

"Um, Sir, that takes them out of bounds on the approach."

"Nonsense. If they can get there, it exists. The rules were slid one way, I'm sliding them back." Keep calm, he told himself. Direction has to be clear and precise and without panic. If you get excited, so will everyone else, and you'll end up with a mob. "Kindly deliver the orders, as quick as you can. Call Squadron 3 back to base. I'm likely to want to commit them soon, and it will be terribly helpful if they were here when I do so."

*****

"What the hell did you steal this time, Peter?" Thomas found himself surprised at his bad language, but it was exasperating how Peter seemed to have taken the Socialist slogan that Property is Theft, and then reversed it.

"A flare gun."

"Why? What use is that? All it will do is tell everyone where we are. Lieutenant Hawkins told us to stay out of sight and shooting flares into the sky that can be seen for miles isn't staying out of sight."

Peter smiled. "Flares are hot. Canvas tents burn."

*****

We are in such trouble, Thomas thought. The four of them stood in front of Colonel Dalkeith's desk, standing at attention while he finished reading some report. Lieutenant Hawkins was standing next to them, as was Sergeant Taylor. Both of them had no expression on their face.

Colonel Dalkeith kept reading the report. No-one said a word. Thomas stared at a spot on the wall one foot above Colonel Dalkeith's head. Eventually, Colonel Dalkeith looked up. He looked each of the Riflemen up and down, slowly.

"Miller, O'Grady, Barry, Grant," he said. "You know, I rather get the impression that I'll be seeing a lot of you four over the coming months. Peacocks, mess silver, and now this. I predict that within a year you will either be hanged or sergeants. Possibly both. Lieutenant Hawkins has explained to me what happened. Major Brampton has explained to me what happened. Colonel de Villiers has explained to me what happened. I'll be fascinated to hear your version. Rifleman Recruit O'Grady?"

"Got the job done, Sir."

"You might say that. I understand your orders were to stop the dragoons using their base of operations."

"That's what we did, Sir." Thomas continued to stare at the spot on the wall.

"You did it by burning it entirely to the ground, causing the horses to stampede in all directions, and some haven't been found yet. One of the tents that got burnt to the ground was their store tent, with saddles and equipment and leatherwork, all of which, surprisingly enough, were also burned. It was only the fact that we've had so much rain that meant that the ground was wet and you didn't burn the fields for ten miles. Anything to say on that?"

"They didn't use the base after that, Sir. Not our fault their tents were too close together."

"Their tents were too close together," Colonel Dalkeith said slowly and meaningfully. "Do you expect me to tell

Colonel de Villiers it was all his fault for putting his tents too close together, and that it had nothing to do with the Riflemen who started the fire?"

"Yes, Sir."

Lieutenant Hawkins spoke quickly. "Sir, Major-General Younghusband did say that if an exercise was to have any value, it had to be taken seriously and simulate potential conditions that might be encountered. It would have been worse had the dragoons done that in Persia."

"How, exactly, might it have been worse?"

"We had a machine gun, Sir," said Windy brightly, making matters worse. "With the squads all around the base, like and all the confusion in the base, it would have been a bloodbath, Sir."

Colonel Dalkeith shook his head. "Have you any idea how much damage you four caused? I calculate that if I stop your pay until the arrears are cleared, it will be nearly a hundred years before you've paid it off." He paused. "That said, you did stop the dragoons from using their base, which were your instructions. I don't know whether to punish you or reward you." He steepled his fingers. "As a result, I'm going to do both. Lieutenant Hawkins, it's fairly clear your platoon needs to be kept out of trouble, and they're clearly accomplished at getting the job done. They've reached the standard of Riflemen, so they're now officially part of the Regiment. I'll speak to you about how you'll fit in to the Regiment. I'm granting the platoon four days' leave. They need to be back here 2359 on Sunday. That's the reward. As for you four gentlemen, Lady Dalkeith is going down to London to sort out a few things. She will need four Riflemen to assist her with fetching and carrying and running messages. I believe that I have found four volunteers."

*****

"You know, Teddie, it was your own fault. Your tents were too close together. Think yourself lucky that this was only an exercise. In the field, you'd be looking at a butcher's bill as well."

*****

"We're going to London by train, Ma'am?"

Lady Dalkeith looked at the four riflemen. "Of course. You don't think we'd travel all that way by car, did you? I don't suppose any of you have travelled first-class before. All you need to do is remember the following. You are representing the Regiment. Colonel Dalkeith will be upset if you let the Regiment down. Everything else flows from that. I expect you will be a credit to the Regiment. I will be doing some shopping in London, and I will be talking to a few people. Is that understood?"

"Yes, Ma'am. Ma'am, why do you need us? Shopping, well, it's not really something you need us for."

"Rifleman O'Grady, it will not be long before the Regiment goes to Persia. The Army will supply us with everything they think we will need. Unfortunately, there will be items that we actually need that are not on the Army's list. This trip is to acquire some of those items. Your presence is required to make sure the items are suitable."

"Why not send a Sergeant, Ma'am? This isn't, well, you're the Colonel's lady."

"Young man, the sergeants are busy making preparations. This is in addition to, not instead of."

"Us, Ma'am? You keep saying us. You're talking as though you'll be going to Persia with the Regiment."

"Of course I will be coming."

"It will be, um, uncomfortable, Ma'am."

"Very probably. Our children are grown up. I will have no duties here when the Regiment travels. I would prefer to be uncomfortable with my husband than comfortable without him. Now, I intend to sleep on the train. I suggest you make sure you have something to amuse yourselves with, quietly, during the trip."

There were only a few people on the platform, and these seemed to be avoiding standing too close to the soldiers. Maybe it was because they'd be using something other than first class. Maybe. Although they seemed to be looking away to avoid any possibility of eye contact.

The train came into the station and waited at the platform. Lady Dalkeith pointed to her luggage, then climbed into a carriage. Thomas looked around, and the other three were nowhere to be seen. Apparently, teamwork and friendship didn't extend to helping him lift luggage into the carriage.

He didn't even dare swear under his breath, as Lady Dalkeith may overhear.

*****

Windy had found a bookseller on the platform. Lady Dalkeith had said they had to be quiet in the carriage, so maybe a book would be a good thing. It wasn't a shop, just a kind of trolley filled with cheap, battered books. The bookseller was a broad-set man with an amazing set of muttonchop whiskers, and a heavy, much-patched jacket. Windy started looking at the books. They were cheap, and not very well cared for.

"What are they about?" he asked.

"No idea, Tommy. I'm no scholar. Thrupence for a book. Penny back if you bring it back."

"Your sign says tuppence."

"Thrupence for you, Tommy." His voice dripped contempt.

They argued for a bit, but it was obvious he was going to be overcharged. He took a book and headed to the carriage. The others had just finished loading Lady Dalkeith's luggage.

He looked around. Peter and Frank weren't here. Windy felt guilty, because it looked like Thomas had been left to do all the work. The others appeared; Frank said he'd been checking on the other compartments in the coach. "I make sure they understand Lady Dalkeith wish to sleep, not want noise." Peter had got distracted by the engine and had been talking to the driver.

They got into the compartment. Two long seats, a window looking out, and a wooden door into the passageway, luggage racks above the seats.

"Before you sit down, get down my blue case. Get the two sheets out from it."

"Yes, ma'am. Why, ma'am?"

"Because soot from the engine gets everywhere. No matter how thoroughly they're cleaned, these seats will have soot engrained in them. You won't want to get soot on your uniforms, and I certainly don't want to get it on my clothes. I always sit facing away from the engine. That way soot blows past me, not into my face. The journey will take three hours and five minutes. I intend to sleep for much of that, and I do not expect any disturbances. I see Rifleman Miller had the foresight to purchase a railway novel."

They settled down, Lady Dalkeith on one seat, facing away from the engine, with the four Riflemen squeezed close on the other seat. The train started with a judder, almost throwing the Riflemen off the seat.

Windy started to read his book. "It's about a highwayman, not a railway," he said, quietly.

"Railway novel," whispered Thomas. "Books to read on a railway journey. You buy one, read it on the journey, throw it away at the end. They're not real books."

"What do you mean, not real books? It's got an author and everything. Did you write this? J O'Grady is the author." Windy showed Thomas the cover.

"No, I did not write a railway novel. They're not very good."

Windy decided to ignore Thomas, and he started to read. He read slowly and carefully. He didn't want to waste his money by reading too quickly. The book had to last the whole trip.

Thomas closed his eyes and tried to think. A lot had happened, and everything had been such a rush. He wondered what his father would think. Would he be missing him? Would he be pretending he'd never had a son? Would he still not understand?

If he looked out of the window, he might be able to see the edge of the grounds. They would have to be passing home sometime. He wondered if the staff had missed him. He then started to wonder why he was thinking about home. He'd not had much time to think during training, always having to rush around and clean and do strange things and drill and more rushing.

His father had assumed he had got one of the servant girls into trouble. It wasn't true, not even close, but it wasn't entirely false. He had dallied with Mary, and she'd said he'd only ever be the son of his father. "If you do well, it will be because of his money or his friends."

The trouble was, she was right. His father had been scouting out suitable positions for him. Not jobs, obviously. Positions. He'd also been scouting out for a suitable wife and organising his life. Making his life as straightforward as possible and making it suitable, until he could take over the estate.

He'd asked her what her plans were. She'd laughed and said that she'd get his father to seduce her, make her his mistress, and then she'd become so indispensable to him that he'd marry her. Then she laughed at him.

"Servants don't get to make plans. They get plans made for them."

He'd said that he would be a success without help from his father, and she had just laughed.

He missed home, although he had hated it there.

"They can't write that!" said Windy suddenly.

"Shh!" said everyone.

"Can't write what?" whispered Thomas.

"This book. They can't write this. It's, wrong."

"How do you mean?"

Windy blushed and continued in an outraged whisper. "The highwayman. He held up a carriage, and the driver ran off, leaving a noblewoman and her daughter. He was going to ravish the daughter, but the noblewoman pleaded with him, and begged him to spare her, so he ravished her instead."

"Can I see?" Frank asked, taking the book. He struggled over some of the words, but he was absorbed by it. "Her clothing disordered, she lay helpless, transfixed by the sight of his rampant masculinity. At first, she whimpered in fear as he knelt over her, and then she started to moan in anguish as he thrust his manhood deep within her, and then the moans of anguish became moans of sheer pleasure as he had his insatiable way with her."

"They can't write that," said Windy. "It's, well, it's indecent."

"It's a railway novel. It's *supposed* to be indecent."

Four very embarrassed soldiers stared at Lady Dalkeith. They hoped desperately that she hadn't heard the passage, and they very much feared that she had.

"It has given me an idea, though." Lady Dalkeith cupped her chin. "They're very educational."

The four soldiers looked at each other. This was not what they expected.

"Educational, Ma'am?" Thomas asked, very cautiously.

"Absolutely. It has long and complicated words, but nonetheless, Riflemen Barry and Miller were reading it avidly. The hardest part of teaching people to read is getting them to want to read. I rather think other soldiers might enjoy these books. Of course, it'll be more effective if they think it's not allowed."

"Ma'am," said Windy thoughtfully. "If we had stake money, we could buy a load out here, and then either sell or rent them in the barracks, and then pay you back." His disgust at the books seemed to now take second place to making money out of them.

Thomas was scandalised.

Lady Dalkeith nodded thoughtfully. "I'll expect a ten per cent profit on a loan. I'll get Garnet to ban them from the barracks. That should increase demand nicely."

Thomas looked out of the window. He was getting involved in selling pornographic literature. What would his father say?

"Indeed, I rather fancy it should be possible to write one of these. Abducting the Harem of the Persian Prince," Lady Dalkeith mused. "I think that might do nicely."

"A bit like the Rape of the Sabine Women, Ma'am?" said Thomas. He couldn't help himself.

"Exactly so. The classics are just pornography with history. Writing it should come naturally to an O'Grady."

"Me, Ma'am?"

"Us. I'm from Boston, remember. My maiden name is O'Grady."

"You want to write a railway novel, Ma'am?" Thomas asked. His brain was having difficulty getting around the concept.

"I think that's an excellent idea."

Thomas looked out of the window. What would his father say?

*****

Peter was excited about the trip by taxi cab out to Croydon airport. He seemed to know all about these vehicles, and he babbled about the Conditions of Fitness, and how this Beardmore design was amazing. It wasn't a particularly comfortable ride, especially as it was a four-seater, and two of those were taken by the driver and Lady Dalkeith. Four soldiers into two seats makes for some uncomfortable mathematics.

The others didn't seem fazed by the sheer number of people in London. Windy and Frank had lived here, and Peter had come into London from time to time on business. Thomas had never felt the need.

The streets were packed and noisy. Cars and buses and pedestrians flew in all directions. People hurried around, head down, with no-one paying any attention to anything around them. Enterprising urchins had set up stalls on road corners and outside shops, selling all manner of things, from flowers to hot chestnuts. Not only urchins, but adults as well, talking cheerfully with a smile on their face that never touched their eyes.

Thomas hoped he would have the chance to see some of the sights. As if on cue, the taxicab turned a corner, and he could see Westminster Abbey. He'd seen pictures of it, but nothing had prepared him for how impressive it was close up. It was enormous, and he stared at the intricate work all the way up. Men were working on the tower, repairing or cleaning something.

"Angels," said Windy. "That's what we call them. They're fixing up some of the bits. Angels because they're working close to God, and Angels because that's what they become if they slip. It's good money they get."

"They don't get more money. They just get it quicker."

"I don't understand, Peter," said Thomas.

"They don't pay you after you fall. So that means they don't pay for so long. They don't pay you any more, they just pay it quicker."

"Doesn't anyone try to make it safer?"

"Why? There are always more Angels. If they complain, they lose their job. If they go into a Union, they lose their job and become known as trouble-maker. And safety costs. It's cheaper just to get another Angel." Peter sounded bitter. "It's the way things are, and it's wrong."

As they drove past the Houses of Parliament, Thomas was deep in thought, and disturbed.

Once they crossed over Westminster Bridge, the city changed. It was no longer a place of work, an ant-hill of industry, but a place where tradesmen lived. Little houses packed close together, each just large enough for a family, neatly kept and showing the signs of a proud, careful, cautious owner. There was a rhythm to the places, with a few shops and a church and houses cramped around a small park, overlapping with a nearly identical place. Like small villages squeezed together and trying to fit into not enough space.

As they drove south, there was a bit more space for these villages, and the houses were slightly bigger, and there were gaps between the houses.

Finally, they drove along a road in a large park, and a man with a red flag waved them to a stop. "Plane about to take off," he explained.

"There's a road running through the middle of an airfield?" Peter sounded incredulous.

"Of course not," said the man. "That would be silly. The road runs between two airfields. Of course, that was when planes were smaller. Now they're bigger, so they need bigger airfields, so the two airfields were combined into one. It's all being sorted out. We'll buy the road and close it. Just needs a few details to sort out."

"Major Tucker is expecting me."

"Ah yes, you must be Lady Dalkeith. The Major told me to keep an eye out for you. He said that since you wanted to talk about his airships, I was to direct you to the airship."

They began to walk to the hanger next to the inflated airship where a swarm of workers poured over the carriage beneath.

"Really, gentlemen, I appreciate your concern, but I hardly think Croydon is a dangerous place."

Thomas looked around. Automatically and without thinking, they had each taken up position with Thomas and Frank in front and to left and right of Lady Dalkeith, and Peter and Windy behind and to left and right. A protective square around Lady Dalkeith, and they'd done it without thinking.

Major Tucker came out to meet them. He walked in a stiff-legged manner, leaning heavily on a cane. He walked quickly, but it wasn't a natural walk.

"Wooden leg," Thomas guessed.

"Jimmy, how are you?" Lady Dalkeith asked.

"Frazzled, fraught, and frustrated, Lady Dalkeith, and delighted to see you."

"You need a Mrs Tucker to deal with frazzled, fraught, and frustrated. Is there a Mrs Tucker yet?"

"I'm still a confirmed bachelor, Ma'am."

"Well, we'll just have to find you the right girl. The Regiment owes you that. Gentlemen, Major Tucker used to be in the Regiment until his injury. It was thought that a one-legged officer wasn't appropriate for field operations and he's too good an officer to cast aside, so we found him a desk job."

"I have my very own captain's chair. Going into action from the comfort of a chair and sheltered from the weather. It's only a training ship, but hopefully there will be proper field work soon."

"Jimmy, the reason I'm here is that the Regiment will soon be going to Persia. There are some Navy airships out there, which we believe will be at our disposal, and we need to know how best to use them."

"Lady Dalkeith, are you implying that regulations and doctrine might not be the best way of using airships?"

"I'm just a weak and silly woman who couldn't possibly grasp the intricacies of such things. The officers of the Regiment understand doctrine perfectly, and they wouldn't dream of questioning it. I'm given to flights of fancy, however."

"And the four riflemen?"

"They're here to test out a little idea of mine. You can fly anywhere you like, and hover over a spot. You could carry riflemen and drop them there, couldn't you? I understand landing could be a problem, so how do you get people down to the ground without the ship coming to the ground?"

"Things are easy. Pack them carefully, toss them out of the door, and Isaac Newton does the rest. People are harder. Parachutes, obviously, but the wind blows them around, and it's hard to get them to land where we want them."

"Are parachutes safe?"

"Absolutely," Major Tucker said. "At least 75 per cent work perfectly."

The four riflemen looked at each other. That wasn't a number they liked.

"What about climbing down a rope?"

"We normally cruise at about half a mile. Clear skies in Persia, so airships will cruise much higher. The higher you are, the father you can see. That's a long rope."

"So how do you get people to the ground?"

"Near the enemy? We don't. We would have to get very low, and the bag is very vulnerable, and it takes time to gain height to get out of range. We can be seen for miles, so they'll see us coming down."

"What about at night?"

"Landing at night? Or at least, getting close to the ground? Risky."

"Is it possible?"

"I'll look into it. The Navy won't like it."

"Good. How do you send messages between ships and to the ground? You can't really send a runner with a message or string a telephone line."

"Signal lamps, Ma'am. Can't use them on the ground, they're too heavy to carry, and they need line of sight, which is a problem when hills get in the way. Those aren't problems in a ship."

"So, you can send messages to people on the ground, but they can't send you messages?"

"Permanent base can send messages, but not troops needing to move."

"Very good. These four riflemen need to be taught how to read signal lamps."

*****

They had worked hard at learning the signalling code. Not only had there been the code for each letter and number, but the signaller had explained how words got shortened to make messages shorter and quicker to send. "Tm 4 T" apparently meant that they were to gather everything up and return to the hanger for a tea break.

All the way on the drive back to the hotel, Lady Dalkeith had quizzed them endlessly about what they had learned.

As they drove up to her hotel, she nodded. "You've worked hard. I will not need you until the morning. Whatever you do tonight, remember that you are representing the Regiment."

They weren't sure what they wanted to do. Free time wasn't something that they were used to. Thomas suggested going to see a play. Frank thought a music hall might be better. Windy wanted something cheap, because he had to send nearly all his money home, and Peter wanted somewhere that would have a lot of people. They solved the problem by cutting cards, and Thomas got to choose. They went to a theatre.

"You'll like Coriolanus. It's about a soldier. He's the best general in the country, and he saves the country many times. People want him to lead the country, but the qualities that make him a great soldier make him a bad politician, and he upsets other politicians. He's too good just to cast aside, and the people like him, so other politicians have him killed, and the changes he was making fall apart."

"Does it have many jokes?" asked Frank. "Or pretty girls?"

"I'm sorry, sir, we don't have any available seats." A doorman from the theatre stood between them and the ticket booth. "There's a music hall not far away."

"But we want to see Coriolanus."

"I'm afraid it's a bit inappropriate, sir. I think you'll find the music hall more suitable."

Thomas got annoyed. "You're surely not worried that we'll force our way back-stage, make off with the actresses, ravish them insatiably, and then sell them into white slavery once our foul lusts have been spent?"

"That's good plan," said Frank, impressed.

For some reason, this didn't help matters. The theatre was adamant that there were no available seats, although the ticket booth remained open.

They gave up and went to the Music Hall. Truth be told, they enjoyed it. They didn't get the disdainful look from people they had been getting used to, and they didn't feel as though they weren't welcome. It was all new to Thomas; a series of short acts, with the compere hustling through things to keep up a breakneck speed. The auditorium was plush and gaudy, but it was showing signs of age. The people watching obviously believed in audience participation, and looking around, they looked like the servants at home when they were dressed up in their best clothes. Commentary from the audience was loud and often pithy; and the innuendo from the compere was met with long suggestive noises from the crowd.

A couple of acts stood out for Thomas. One was what was billed as "Lion Comiques," with the performer dressed, not as one of the lower class, but as a gentleman preparing for a night out, boasting of the conquests that he'd made and that he would make. What stuck in Thomas' mind was a phrase from the song: "I'll ask their consent, and they daren't say no; for they know if they say no I'll let them go, with no word, so they never say no, and I'm an irresistible chap." The disturbing part was he'd never seen it like that. He was also disturbed at the portrayal of the gentleman; an idler, casual about leaving destruction in their wake, regarding serving women as disposable commodities.

The second act that caught his attention was a song by Marie Lloyd, which seemed to be about a family leaving rented accommodation during the night, packing their belongings into a van, and the daughter having to follow the van, but getting lost. The song said that she asked a constable for help, with unfortunate consequences.

The third act that took his notice was towards the end of the show. Thomas didn't understand at first. It was a sketch between a sergeant and a rifleman, but nothing much seemed remarkable about them, other than that they'd done a pretty good job of finding the right uniforms so quickly. The rifleman looked and had gestures just like Windy, so obviously they had copied those, which was quick work, but Thomas still couldn't see the joke.

"They lady impersonators," whispered Frank. "They copy Windy good."

They did, and the sergeant looked like a sergeant. They both had the gestures and stance. Thomas couldn't believe they were women.

The young recruit is silly – 'e thinks o' suicide.
'E's lost 'is gutter-devil; 'e 'asn't got 'is pride;

But day by day they kicks 'im, which 'elps 'im on a bit,
Till 'e finds 'isself one mornin' with a full an' proper kit.

The cruel-tyrant-sergeants they watch 'im 'arf a year;
They watch 'im with 'is comrades, they watch 'im with 'is beer;
They watch 'im with the women at the regimental dance,
And the cruel-tyrant-sergeants send 'is name along for "Lance."

"Do you think Sergeant Taylor will put Windy's name forward for Lance?" Peter asked.

One of the staff handed Windy a note. He read it and looked worried. "They've asked me to go backstage after the show."

"That good," said Frank. "Maybe you do well."

"I can't go. What if they, you know."

"Then we'll collect you in the morning," said Peter.

"Can you come with me? Just in case, you know."

"They asked for you, not for us."

"Yes, but we're a squad, we stick together."

"You're going to have a strange wedding night when you get married," said Peter.

"It good idea," said Frank. "We must stick together. It important we protect Windy from actresses." He grinned. "Maybe we take them back to barracks with us."

Backstage was a tiny room, which wasn't large enough for all of them to go in. Peter, Frank and Thomas had to stand in the corridor, stepping aside as the staff were trying to pack things away. They could just about hear the conversation in the room.

"Sorry about copying you, ducks. Soldiers and sailors are always a success, and you've got such precise movements. You were a natural for us. To show we're sorry, we'll let you buy us dinner."

"I'm afraid I don't have much money," Windy stammered.

"He doesn't have much money, Beryl."

"He *says* he doesn't have much money, Iris."

"Are you really a rifleman?"

"He looks like a rifleman."

"But he's so young, more like a rifleboy."

"Do you think he could teach us about riflemen?"

"Possibly, Beryl, possibly."

"But he's got no money, Iris."

"Maybe he can pay in kind. Young man, could you show us how to march like soldiers, because if you can, the Hall will pay for dinner."

"What about my friends?"

"We'll see."

When they came out into the corridor, Thomas saw that the two actresses were a lot older than they seemed when they were on stage. Beryl, the sergeant, was a solidly-built red-haired lady, with long sideburns. On looking closely, Thomas saw that the sideburns were hair that had been stuck on, but which looked real to anything other than a close inspection. Iris was smaller, about Windy's size, a blonde with tied-back hair. Both had to be in their 30s. Maybe older, Thomas wasn't very good at guessing the age of women.

"Enough for a platoon," said Beryl. "You're gorgeous impressionists. You all look just like real soldiers."

"We are real soldiers," said Thomas.

"Ducks, there's a place that does a good dinner that's happy to have accomplished artistes dine there, but wouldn't let a real soldier darken its doors. So just pretend to be a real soldier and not be a real soldier, and you might get a good meal."

"You are saying we should pretend to be pretending to be soldiers?"

"Think you can manage that?"

"Not sober," muttered Frank. "It wrong."

"Are you Italian?" asked Beryl.

"No! Sicilian, not Italian."

"No! Sicilian, not Italian," Beryl repeated, copying the tone.

"Come along and uphold the honour of the Regiment," Iris added.

That was how they came to be in a small place off Silver Street. It didn't have a name, and it seemed to be a jumble of small rooms that were somehow connected. It was busy, there was what seemed to be a bar, and there were small tables where people were eating. Crowds of people jostled for space, sawdust covered the floor, and above the bar was a sign that read: "No Solders or Irish."

"Evening, Butch," Beryl said. "Bottle of the Pope's telephone number."

"Expanding the troop?" the barman asked. "I don't know. They're not so convincing as you and Irish." He reached beneath the bar and handed over a bottle of whisky and half a dozen glasses. "You're the only person who asks for this."

They crowded around a table in a corner. Beryl and Iris, who used the names Barry and Irish when they were in costume, sat either side of Windy against the wall.

"The Pope's telephone number?" Thomas asked.

Irish pointed to the bottle. "VAT 69. Stage humour. Now, we want you to teach us phrases you actually use."

It was hard to explain over the noise. It was even harder because some of the language wasn't suitable for the ears of a lady, no matter how much they looked like Riflemen. Windy coughed and spluttered when he drank some of the whisky.

"Why didn't you pay for the drink?" he asked once he had recovered. "And why do you come here?"

"We come here because we get to see how men act and talk and stand. As for not paying, a soldier never tells."

Then a group of cavalrymen came in. Loud and braying; just rankers, but they cast an air of entitlement about them.

"The sign says no soldiers," Peter asked. "Why are they allowed in?"

"Because they not real soldiers," Frank replied. Unfortunately, he said it when there was a natural lull in talk around the place, and his voice could be heard clearly.

The cavalrymen made their way across. "Bit rich coming from your actresses," said the tallest. Five cavalrymen.

"Remember what Lady Dalkeith said," hissed Thomas.

Frank shrugged. "Real soldiers go to battle. Pretty tin soldiers for Pall Mall soldiering, proper soldiers for Persia."

"Beryl, you'd best tell your girls to mind their tongues."

"You know, Irish," said Beryl, "we've not studied how this looks like it will turn out."

"Credit to the Regiment," hissed Thomas, desperate to stop a fight breaking out.

"You girls could get a place in the Rifles. There's only one man in that regiment, and that's Lady Dalkeith. But I'll tell you what, give us a kiss and a cuddle, and we'll say no more about it." The cavalryman said this last to Windy.

"You'd not get what you thought you'd bargained for," said Peter.

"Spoils of war, boys?"

"I think my girls are more like men than you riders are." Iris sounded amused.

The four riflemen stood up and turned to face the five cavalrymen.

"They stand like girls."

Thomas noticed Frank slipping something over the knuckles of his right hand, and Peter leaned on a chair, hands gripping the top.

"Windy, get the ladies out of the way. We don't want any trouble," Thomas said.

"Wendy, now there's a pretty name. Are you really going to act like you want a fight? Admire your dedication to your craft, but you know how it would turn out. It's not like you're like the real Colonel of the greenbellies, that horse Lady Dalkeith."

"You not call Lady Dalkeith whore," said Frank, hitting the man on the jaw. Peter picked up the chair, and after that, things became confused.

*****

Thomas groaned and held his head. It throbbed, and his mouth felt dry, and his tongue didn't seem to fit in his mouth. His uniform was a mess, he seemed to have tunic buttons grasped in his hand, only they were bright and shiny, and not Rifleman black. His face hurt, and things were a bit blurry when he opened his eyes.

His eye. One of his eyes didn't seem to want to open, and it hurt. He touched it gingerly. It felt larger than the other, and painful to touch.

His knuckles hurt, and he saw that he had a lot of cuts and bruises. He stood up, and his ribs ached. Frank and Peter were in the room, and both of them looked the worse for wear. Torn uniforms. Peter had a bruise that covered half of his face.

The door was just bars, the walls thick and whitewashed, and there were no windows. In the corner of the room was a noisome bucket.

The smell hit Thomas, and he went from feeling sick to being sick. Luckily, he had just enough time to get to the bucket. Unluckily, that meant the smell struck him full force, and he was sick again. He could feel sweat on his brow, and he shook like a leaf in a breeze. He retched again, and again, and his legs felt weak, and his head throbbed. He guessed that he must have eaten something that was off.

There was a rattle on the door, and it was opened by a policeman.

"All right, my lovely lads. Someone has come to collect you. Get up and bring your things with you."

Windy had come to collect them, Thomas thought. They were led past a couple of other cells.

"Oi. You. Empty the bucket." The policeman indicated Frank, who scowled, and then smiled, and collected the bucket without a murmur.

"No!" said Thomas as they passed another cell. This one had five cavalrymen in it, and he could see Frank preparing to empty the bucket into the cell. "We want to get out."

"He not say where I empty bucket."

"Let's just get out of here before we get into trouble."

The police sergeant at the front desk was talking. Unfortunately, he wasn't talking to Windy, but to Lady Dalkeith. She looked at the three riflemen, who all tried to hide behind each other and avoid being seen.

"*Before* you get into trouble, Rifleman O'Grady? I would be fascinated to learn what you would regard as actually getting into trouble. Where is Rifleman Miller?"

"He take ladies to safety, Ma'am," said Frank.

"And he hasn't yet returned," said Lady Dalkeith. "I dread to think how safe they are. I suspect that they are as safe as you are not in trouble. Rifleman Grant, could you kindly explain what happened?"

"We went to a music hall, Ma'am."

There was a silence as Lady Dalkeith waited for him to continue, while Peter felt he'd said all that needed to be said.

"Rifleman Grant, I don't actually *need* to get you released. I can call your Lieutenant Hawkins and explain your predicament, and he would have to draw the Colonel's attention to the situation, and he will not be happy. I do need to know what happened."

"We talked to a couple of performers and took them out to dinner."

"I see. Rifleman O'Grady, I understand that you went to an establishment that clearly and specifically said no Irish and no soldiers."

"I'm not Irish, Ma'am."

"You wear the name O'Grady, and you're not Irish?"

"Duke of Wellington was born in Ireland, Ma'am, but he wasn't Irish."

"Being born in a stable doesn't make one a horse. I know. It also doesn't make one Jesus. What happened next, Rifleman Barry?"

"Cavalrymen came, insulted ladies, insulted Regiment, and insulted you. So, we uphold honour of ladies, Regiment, and you, Ma'am."

"You got into a bar-room brawl. What happened next?"

"Windy, that is, Rifleman Miller, escorted the ladies to safety, Ma'am," said Thomas. He remembered that part. "We defended the honour of those who had been insulted."

"And then?"

"Then the police arrived," said Peter. "They tried to break up the fight. Well, we weren't finished with the fight, and neither were the cavalry, so we joined forces against the common foe. Then the police sent more, so we, um,"

"We made a strategic withdrawal, Ma'am." Thomas was starting to remember bits. "Us and the cavalry."

"Then we go to another place where we can uphold honour. But we thirsty and they thirsty, so we have some drinks first."

"Them some stevedores came and tried to throw us out, so we threw them out. Then we agreed with the cavalrymen to settle things in Hyde Park, where we wouldn't damage things. But when we got there, there was a lot of police there, on account of the demonstration, so we finds a quiet corner."

"Only it turn out not be quiet. Some people were,"

"Bird watching," said Thomas quickly. "A gentleman and his companion were bird watching."

"Bird watching? At night?"

"Owls, Ma'am. They were watching owls," Thomas said desperately.

"Only we not notice them at first, and they call police, and the police bring us here."

"And Rifleman Miller?"

"Yes, Ma'am?" Rifleman Miller entered the station with two women. They looked familiar to Thomas. They were dressed as ladies. A bit over-dressed, but maybe that was the fashion in London.

"Rifleman Miller, would you explain your role in this?"

"Not much to tell, Ma'am. When the trouble started, I escorted Miss Bannerman and Miss Wallace to safety."

"Safety?"

"Yes, Ma'am. I escorted them home and saw them safely inside."

"But we was scared the cruel soldiers might have followed us, so he kindly offered to stay with us and protect us."

"And the good Rifleman told us how all the other Riflemen called him a boy."

"Well, one thing's for sure, he ain't a boy."

"Not now, Beryl, not now."

"And he teaches us an extraordinary way of presenting arms, and we just had to fall in. But now we've found your friends, ducks, we'll leave you and we'll try and get some sleep, you naughty boy."

"Beryl, don't forgets."

"Of course. We guessed you might need some uniforms." She handed over a box that had Riflemen uniforms in. "You take care, ducks, remember what we teaches you, and look us up next time you're in town."

Once the ladies had left, Lady Dalkeith steepled her fingers. "Let me see if I understand correctly. You got into a bar-room fight with members of the Household Cavalry, in a bar that you were specifically excluded from. You caused considerable damage, and then you got into a fight with the police. One of you absconded with not one, but two actresses, and had what I believe the railway novelists would call his insatiable lustful way with them both. Meanwhile, you others get drunk, get into another fight, disturb a gathering, disturb a gentleman and his companion while they were bird-watching, get into another fight with members of the Household Cavalry, and get into another fight with the police. Your uniforms are now a disgrace, and you disturbed my sleep when I was called to sort things out. Tell me, did you uphold the Honour of the Regiment?"

"Well, Ma'am, that is," Thomas stumbled.

"No prevarication. A simple yes or no. Did you win your fight with the Household Cavalry?"

*****

"I will return later," said Lady Dalkeith. "I expect to hear good reports of you. Sister, you know what I expect from them."

And that was that. They had been left in the London Hospital, and they were standing in front of a diminutive woman of middle-age, almost as broad as she was tall, who wore the crisp uniform of a nursing sister. The redoubtable Sister Luckes, who had been in charge of training nurses at the London Hospital for many a year.

"Aye, first thing thee'll keep in mind is that my nurses have a job to do, and if thee distracts any with tha wanton ways, Lady Dalkeith will ha' a bad report on thee from me, and the nurse that thee distracts will be out o' a job wi' na reference. Thee's here to learn, and that is just what thee will be. Mind your manners, and we'll get along fine. Not, and then not."

"Sister, what exactly are we here to learn?" Thomas asked. His head wasn't hurting quite so much.

"Not nursing, that's siccar. Thee's here to lug and carry and assist my nurses."

"Yes, Sister, that's what we're to do here, but what are we supposed to be learning?"

"Ach, thee's none too smart, for all tha smooth voice. Thee will get used to the sight o' wounded bodies. Thee will no do too well if tha faints at the first sight o' blood when first under fire in Persia. If tha' faints here when seeing a body wi' inside bits on the outside, it's no big deal. Do that in Persia, and tha' comrades may die as a result. It's that simple.

"Now, thee's to learn, and tha'll no do that together, so thee will each be working wi' a nurse, and mind what I said about minding tha' manners and no dallying wi' my nurses, who ha' better things to do wi' their time. Is that all understood?"

Ten minutes later, Thomas was walking briskly, trying to keep up with his allocated nurse. Nurse Charrington was brisk, a young woman with too many freckles across her face beneath her eyes to be called pretty, but she had a soft, gentle voice. He expected her to have a fiery temper, because she had red hair, but she seemed very patient, even if she did walk briskly.

"When you're walking, you're not nursing," she explained. "Nurses nurse, not stroll about in the park. Keep up."

She was also too muscled and strong to be elegant or lady-like. Thomas quickly worked out why when she showed him how to make a bed, and the amount of lifting and carrying that was required. After half an hour, Thomas was starting to feel the effort, but Nurse Charrington didn't seem to be struggling.

Then it was time to make sure everything was ready for when the doctor came and did his rounds. Naturally, two minutes before the doctor was due to arrive, one of the patients started shouting and throwing things, and screaming about invisible spiders tormenting him and how he had to fight them, and he tried to stagger across to Nurse Charrington, spitting and swearing and with fists clenched.

Thomas stepped in front of the man, grabbed his arms, twisted him round, and walked him back to his bed.

"Be a good gentleman and lie quietly."

"There are the spiders. Giant spiders."

"That's why I'm here. I'm here to deal with the spiders and I can't do that if you get in the way. Be a good gentleman and lie still and quiet while I do my job."

The man was quiet after that. He was an old man, or at least, a man who looked old, with all the signs of a lifetime of heavy drinking.

"I did not need you to protect me," Nurse Charrington said. "I've dealt with worse before."

"I know that, but I wanted to make sure you had time to get everything squared away before the doctor does his inspection."

Nurse Charrington gave a brief half-smile that was gone almost as soon as it appeared, and Thomas felt strangely pleased.

"That's all right then," she said. "I'm not a helpless, frivolous nothing of a lady. I do a job and I do it well."

Thomas was silent for a moment. For an instant, he had a passing thought, wondering what it would be like to have a dalliance with someone as solid as Nurse Charrington. No, not a dalliance. Nurse Charrington was not a dalliance sort of person. He wanted to see her smile again.

"And stop wool-gathering," Nurse Charrington said sharply. "We've a lot to do before rounds."

"I'm supposed to be getting used to the sight of blood and injuries," Thomas said.

"And after rounds, I'll be on duty in emergency. I needed to see if you were to be trusted there first. You'll do."

Somehow, Thomas thought this was high praise and he felt like smiling inside.

He didn't feel like smiling ten minutes later, when the doctor came. A be-whiskered mature man with a scowl and a glare at Thomas.

"Who authorised gutter sweepings to come onto my ward?"

"Sister Luckes, doctor," Nurse Charrington replied.

The doctor snorted. "Women just aren't capable of making a rational decision. Always swayed by emotion. They need guidance and direction from a masculine mind."

Thomas practised his stone-faced expressionless look, because he knew that debating the point might not be wise. He wondered what Lady Dalkeith would say, and that thought made keeping a straight face difficult.

The rounds were surprisingly brief. The doctor glanced at each patient, checked the notes, and muttered something inaudible.

"Ward should be neater. Notes are a disgrace," the doctor said before sweeping out. Nurse Charrington let out a deep breath and relaxed a little. She spoke with another nurse, and then led the way off of the ward.

"Dr Talbot is more relaxed in the afternoon," Nurse Charrington said. "We're going to the accident ward. It's been raining, so we'll get a number of slip injuries. Your job will be to help fetch and carry. Do not try treatments unless you have been told what to do. Is that clear?"

"Yes, Nurse," he said, amused at the note of command in her voice.

"Repeat it back to me so that I know you understood. That's basic procedure."

"My job is to carry things as directed, not to attempt any treatment because I am not trained and the nurses and doctors are, and that I am to do exactly what I'm told."

"That's good," she said and again gave a half-smile that disappeared almost before it appeared. That made Thomas feel unaccountably cheerful.

Then things got busy. At first it was broken legs and obvious cuts. It was busy, but there was nothing too serious.

That changed. There was a hubbub outside, and the doors pushed open. People struggled in with a stretcher, with a man on it. They seemed to having difficulty with getting an iron railing sticking up from the stretcher through.

Then Thomas realised that the railing was sticking through the man on the stretcher, who screamed with pain every time the railing touched a wall or ceiling. Blood was flowing everywhere. The men holding the stretcher looked confused; Thomas realised they didn't know how to put the stretcher down.

Thomas grabbed two chairs, and put them facing each other, about six feet apart.

"You can put him down there," he said, and then he looked at the man, who had an iron railing sticking through his stomach. He felt his knees go weak, and he felt cold and dizzy. He gritted his teeth and the room steadied again. He didn't feel well, but he wasn't in danger of fainting. Nurse Charrington readied the man's arm so that a doctor could administer an injection; the man fell asleep and was carried into another room.

"Are you all right, Rifleman O'Grady?"

Thomas was pleased to hear a note of concern in her voice. "Yes, of course. Is that normal? How does a lady …" His voice faded away as he realised what he was about to say might not have been appreciated.

"Good. Get a mop and get this mess cleaned up. Can't have the room like this."

The rest of the shift was busy, but there were no other terrible injuries. His feet were starting to hurt, as were his shoulders, and he was almost glad to see Lady Dalkeith arrive.

"Make sure everything is cleaned away," Nurse Charrington said. While he cleared away, Lady Dalkeith spoke with Nurse Charrington. He wasn't trying to listen, really he wasn't, but one tends to hear one's own name when it's mentioned in conversation.

"Satisfactory," Nurse Charrington said. "He struggled with a bad one, but he held it together. Yes, satisfactory."

"Good. Rifleman O'Grady, wait here while I collect the others."

Thomas squared his shoulders. As soon as Lady Dalkeith had gone, he went to speak with Nurse Charrington.

"Thank you for the lessons." He took a deep breath, unsure why he was feeling a little nervous. "Perhaps I could buy you dinner as a proper thank you?"

She gave another little half-smile that softened her face, just for an instant. "But Rifleman O'Grady, I am given to understand that you will be leaving for Persia soon. I'm not sure it would be appropriate to dine knowing that you will soon be leaving for foreign parts."

Thomas knew that she was right, but his heart felt heavy. "Of course. Thank you for your lessons. I hadn't realised how much hard work was involved in being an angel."

"Rifleman O'Grady, there's no need to look glum. If we are fated to meet again, then we will meet again, even if you are going half-way round the world."

*****

Lady Dalkeith had promised them a treat, as she was satisfied with what they had done so far. The trouble was that her idea of what a treat was at odds with theirs. They would have liked a music hall or a theatre or dining or a pleasure cruise or a trip to a market or even looking around a museum.

"Markets tomorrow. Dinner tonight. Treat now."

"But Ma'am, it's just a State School. Just orphans and the abandoned."

"Exactly. We will speak to the Headteacher, and then you will have your treat."

It wasn't a pretty school. Grim and foreboding and grey. It more like a prison than anything else.

They paused at the Memorial walls just inside the gate. Dozens of names, and at this school, there were two walls. On the left, a long list of names of soldiers and sailors, with a date, a place and a regiment or ship. Thomas now knew enough to recognise that the regiments named were deployable regiments, not fashionable HSO regiments. No HSO regiments at all. There wouldn't be. These regarded themselves as an elite and would never recruit from a State School. Household Guards and ceremonial troops. Home Service Only. They believed they were an elite, because they served the King, protected the King, and other regiments merely fought for him.

Of course, anyone with money or influence or connections went into HSO regiments, to be near the King and the reins of influence. That meant that HSO regiments had first call on pay and supplies and equipment, because those with money and influence ensured that was the case, because it was important the elite regiments maintain their standards. The fighting regiments got whatever was left.

On the right was another wall, much smaller, but still long. Of nurses and cooks and telegraphic operators, names of girls who had died in far-away lands.

Thomas still didn't see how this was a treat. State Schools took those who had no-one, and taught them to serve the country, and this service was their payment for this education. That was how it worked.

As they were being shown the way to meet the Headmaster, they were aware of an excited whispering following them, and wide eyes of children watching carefully.

"Real Riflemen," whispered one of the children. "First in, last out."

The four riflemen stood a little taller and straighter as they walked. As they passed a small knot of children ranging in ages from five to about fourteen, Windy spoke crisply. "Eyes Right."

Automatically, they did so, and the children clapped their hands in pleasure at being saluted.

"Front."

"Who the Hell promoted you?" grumbled Peter.

"Which of us has been a sergeant, even if it was just for dragoons? Which of us is slated for lance?"

"By actresses, Windy. Actresses can't give promotions." Peter sounded exasperated.

"Which of us spent a night in cells, and which of us spent a night with the actresses?"

"Yes, and bunk mates share. Two actresses is just being greedy."

Frank whispered to Thomas: "Those two always argue like married couple."

"I guess being a bunk mate is a bit like being married," Thomas replied. "In each other's pocket all the time."

"We not argue."

"Frank, that's because I never listen to you."

Luckily, they reached the Headmaster's room before the arguments went any further, and the Headmaster greeted them warmly. He was a man old before his time, careworn and worried, wearing a clean suit that had seen many years of service. Such hair as remained was grey and thin. His desk was strewn with papers, and the actual surface of the desk could not be seen anywhere.

"Lady Dalkeith, a pleasure. Gentlemen."

"Mr Roberts," said Lady Dalkeith. "As I explained in my letter, these gentlemen would like to impart their knowledge of what training for the Uniform entails. In their short time, they have acquired a number of tales. Your older boys might benefit."

A look passed over the face of each Rifleman that clearly said that this was the first they had heard of it.

"That's very considerate of you. It'll be arranged straight away." He glanced out of the window, causing Thomas and the others to do likewise. A car had pulled up, and a girl was being shown into the back. Fair-haired, possibly fifteen years old, and she gave a single glance back at the school. She was scared and trying unsuccessfully not to show it.

Mr Roberts turned his head back with a sigh, and if anything, looked a little older. "If you will pardon the presumption, Lady Dalkeith, this establishment, well, the cost of upkeep is significantly greater than the allowance we receive."

"I do not believe in charity, sir. I am happy to ensure that the less fortunate have the means to assist themselves, but charity alone leads to indolence."

"Of course. I apologise for my presumption in asking."

He led the way towards a class, with younger children walking to other classes, all staring at the Riflemen. They were all, if not starving, at least looking like they could do with a square meal. Boys and girls.

"Girls here as well?" asked Lady Dalkeith.

"There are just as many girl orphans as boy orphans. There aren't enough schools here to keep them separate."

"Doesn't that cause," Lady Dalkeith paused, searching for the right word. "Distractions."

Mr Roberts sighed. "To an extent, but we do have remedies and we keep them too busy for distractions."

Frank snorted, but the snort turned into a cough when Lady Dalkeith's head made a slight movement.

Thomas took the opportunity of this to speak with Peter. "All right," he whispered. "What did you snag from his desk?"

Peter scowled. "I don't steal every chance I get."

Thomas thought about this. "Yes, you do, actually. And you didn't say no, which means you did. What did you steal?"

Peter shrugged. "This letter. Posh paper, good penmanship. It's from money. Not had a chance to read it yet."

Thomas took it. If Peter had been seen snagging it, he could be searched, and it would be really bad if the letter was found. Thomas knew he was much less likely to be suspected. He also wished Peter wouldn't steal absolutely anything that he could, whether it had value or not.

They were shown into a class of forty or so children, mostly 14 and 15 years old. The children sat straight and paid close attention, clearly drilled. They were well-scrubbed, but the clothes they wore were generally badly fitting and had no consistency of colour. Half of the children had no shoes. The eyes of both boys and girls were firmly on the Riflemen.

Mr Roberts introduced Lady Dalkeith, who introduced Rifleman Miller, who was closest in age to the children. "In a year's time, one of you boys could be where Rifleman Miller is now," she said.

Windy started talking about training, hesitantly at first, almost in a whisper. His voice became more confident as he spoke, and he told the children about the field exercise. He had started to explain about the incident with the theft of the mess silver of the dragoons, but Lady Dalkeith shook her head slightly.

While Windy was talking, Thomas read the letter. The first time he read it, he was confused. The second time he read it, he was shocked. The third time he read it, he was angry.

He felt a tap on his shoulder. Lady Dalkeith held out her hand to see the letter. She read it. She pursed her lips. Windy's presentation faded as he became aware of the disturbance behind him.

"Now, children," Lady Dalkeith said. "Tomorrow, we shall return. For the present, I have something to discuss with the Headmaster." She led the way back to the Headmaster's room, not a word being said on the way back, and a chilly atmosphere. Once in the room, she looked sternly at Mr Roberts.

"I require an explanation." She held out the letter.

"I'm caught between Scylla and Charybdis."

Lady Dalkeith read the letter aloud. "It is from Sir Albert Sarahun. He confirms that he has sent his annual banker's draft for the school, and he will send a car. He says it is being sent for a fair-haired maid aged 13-15, of clean limbs and comely features and that the usual procedures will be followed. Explain, sir."

To his credit, Mr Roberts didn't prevaricate. "The banker's draft is sufficient to pay for five children. Without it, five children will remain on the streets, with all that follows. I can save one child, at the cost of five. Or I can save five children, at the cost of one."

"I see." She turned to the Riflemen. "Gentlemen, I shall be staying here for the afternoon, inspecting the school. I shall not need you here. You are at liberty for the next three hours. You may use the taxi car. Listen carefully. You know my position within the Regiment. Very well. I absolutely forbid you to go to the house of Sir Albert Sarahun, and you will absolutely not enter that house, nor will you rescue the girl there. Under no circumstances are you to trouble yourself over the fate of a mere orphan girl. Those are my official instructions based upon my formal position within the Regiment. Do I make myself clear?"

"But, Ma'am," said Windy.

Thomas kicked him into silence, and Peter nodded.

"Chain of Command, Ma'am. Very important."

"Exactly so, Rifleman Grant. Might I add as a word of advice that you remember the first commandment of a soldier on detached freelance duty."

"Very good, Ma'am." The four left quickly.

"First commandment?" Frank asked as soon as they were clear.

"Don't get caught," said Peter.

*****

"We need to see Beryl and Iris first," said Windy.

"For God's sake," said Peter, exasperated. "Sport comes after work."

Windy blushed. "That wasn't what I meant. But Riflemen uniforms are recognisable. 'Police officer, it was a soldier in a green uniform.' How many Riflemen are there in London at the moment? I would guess four. If we go in wearing these, if we get seen, people know it was us even if they don't catch us."

"Well, that's all right, I suppose," said Peter, grudgingly.

Beryl and Iris were pleased to see them. "Ducks, we've got just the thing. Pirates of Penzance. We're including that in the show."

"Pirates?"

"No, ducks, policemen. No-one'll think twice about a couple of coppers. Take your real uniform, change after the deed, and in the worst case, they're looking for three coppers rather than four riflemen."

Thomas picked up on the important word. "Three policemen?"

"Only got three uniforms. It's not a problem. We can dress one of you up as a lady. Thomas, you're way too tall and broad-shouldered. Peter's got a moustache, which isn't a good look for a lady, and Frank's got too many scars. It'll have to be lustful Windy."

"I don't know," said Thomas. "A soldier pretending to be a woman?"

"If we girls can impersonate soldiers, I'm sure a soldier can impersonate a lady."

"I'm not sure." Thomas wasn't convinced. Windy might look like a boy, but he was too strong to be a lady. Not that he was massively strong, but he could keep going on route marches in full kit, and no lady could do that.

"We'll dress him up and you can see what you think. We're good at this, so don't worry. Look how easy we does it the other way."

"This isn't going to work," said Windy plaintively.

"That's exactly the tone of voice, ducks."

Five minutes later, an embarrassed and reluctant Windy emerged, transformed.

"You know, if I didn't know better," said Peter slowly, "I'd ask if I could walk out with you."

Windy did look a picture: not tall, but standing straight, with a slight demure blush. His boyish looks could easily be mistaken for those of a lady.

"This is ridiculous," he said, slamming a palm on a table in a most unladylike manner, destroying the vision.

"I don't know, up until then, I was convinced," said Thomas. "You just have to think about getting the job done. And, if you do really well, maybe Peter will ask you if he could walk out with you when this is over."

Windy responded with a phrase no lady would utter.

"I not convinced," said Frank. "He not that convincing."

"More of the tom-boy, ducks. You're a girl who wanted to do boy games, all athletic and adventuresome, but you've just gone from being a girl to a coltish woman, caught in the transition."

"It'll do," said Thomas. "People will see the dress, and they won't see that it's a boy, if they don't get too close."

"I think you'd look better with your hair loose," said Peter.

"Shut up," said Windy, or words to that general effect.

"No," said Frank. "Not loose hair. Make him look like night lady."

"And that would be perfect," said Thomas. "We know that Sir Sarahun is inclined that way."

As they drove there, they planned. "Quite simple. Peter and Windy, or Wendy, go to the front door and keep people talking. Frank and I will find a back entrance and slip inside, find the girl, and slip out."

Their first problem came at the gate to the grounds. Solid iron railing gates that swung inward to a large lawn and an imposing house beyond. Unfortunately, there was a crowd at the gate. The reason for this soon became evident. A lady had handcuffed herself to the gates, blocking the entrance. She had a sign saying "Votes for Women," and she was creating a disturbance.

"That was quick," said someone. "We only just called you."

"We like to be prompt," said Thomas smoothly. "What seems to be the trouble?"

The crowd approved. That was the sort of question that they expected, asking the blatantly obvious.

"German spies are trying to dig in to steal the Crown Jewels," said a wag in the crowd.

"Very droll," Thomas said.

"Thomas Cavendish?" asked the handcuffed woman. "Aren't you supposed to be dead? Killed in a train accident?"

Thomas stared open-mouthed. "Millicent? Weren't you supposed to be getting married? What are you doing here?"

"I'm taking flying lessons, you silly boy. As I recall, you offered to teach me to fly in your father's hay loft. Why are you a policeman?"

The crowd was settling down to enjoy this entertainment. It was even better than the new talking films. There were a few boos when Peter interrupted.

"Better than a life of crime, Ma'am. You two take Lady Wendy to the house. I'll deal with the lady here."

"Votes for Women!" Millicent shouted as Peter began undoing the handcuffs.

"Ma'am, it's actions like this that prove women aren't fitted to vote. Ask nicely and reasonably, and people may realise you'll use a vote wisely. Act like this, and all you do is upset people. It's not like women are the only people without the vote, and it's not like you can't get what you want when you're rich, woman or man."

"You oaf."

There was just enough room for Thomas, Frank, and Windy to squeeze past, leaving Peter to deal with Millicent.

"I suppose you're going to arrest me and frogmarch me down to the station," shouted Millicent, sitting down on the ground to make this hard.

"I don't think there's any need for that."

Meanwhile, the three moved towards the house. "Flying lessons in a hayloft?" Frank asked.

"Millicent is not a scholar," Thomas said. "New plan. I'll go with Windy to the front door and make the distraction. Frank, sneak in and look around. Be quick. Time's against us."

"I demand that you arrest me and demonstrate the brutality of a male-run society."

"That would mean a lot of paperwork."

Nearer the house, Thomas sighed. Millicent had always been such a shy, demure, innocent girl. Still, the worst was over. Nothing else could go wrong. Frank made his way around the back, and Thomas rang the doorbell.

*****

Frank thought about using an open window. No, he was a policeman. The tradesman's entrance. He just needed to wait until he heard the distraction at the front door. He waited.

And waited.

And waited.

Something had gone wrong. Should he go back and see what? No, his part of the job was to go in and get the girl. He would wait one more minute, and then go in regardless.

Still nothing. He opened the door and walked in to the scullery. No-one was there. This was unexpected. He heard a door open at the front, but other than that, nothing. Into a kitchen. The stove was warm, but there was no-one around. Pans with potatoes in, ready to put on the stove, but no-one to be seen.

He heard Thomas call from the front of the house. "Anyone home?"

Frank moved into the hallway. Big set of stairs going up, and two sets of small stairs going down. One set of stairs down had a locked door. Frank didn't have Peter's facility with opening locks. However, he did have a pair of sturdy, heavy boots, and he had a powerful leg. A single kick broke the door lock.

He started to go down the stairs into the dark. There was a strong smell of dog. He didn't like this one bit, so he took out his favourite knife.

*****

Thomas had rung the doorbell three times, and there had been no answer. He tried to open the door. It was locked.

"Let me," said Windy. "Peter's been teaching me."

It was odd to watch someone who almost looked like a lady behave in such an unladylike way. Windy opened the door. No-one was on the other side. This was strange. They moved through the hallway and looked into each room.

Nothing. No-one was around.

There was a big sweeping staircase leading up. Paintings on the walls, all looking normal. Uncertain what to do, they went up the stairs. Portraits along the walls at the top of the stairs, but some of these didn't seem normal. Some of them had "Monster" painted across them. Mostly across portraits of women.

Thomas gritted his teeth. This was looking bad. He wasn't sure what it was exactly that was bad, but he didn't like this one bit. Windy was looking grim. It was confusing seeing him dressed like a woman; he made him feel as though he should be protecting her, him, instead of letting her, him go into what could be danger.

There was a noise from behind a door at the end. It sounded like a woman beating a carpet. There was nothing else to do but investigate. Thomas turned the handle of the door and opened it slowly.

It was a main bedroom, with a large four-poster bed surrounded by curtains. An open brightly coloured Gladstone bag sat on the foot of the bed. A patterned carpet was hanging from the top of the support, and a portly, well-muscled man, starting to get old, was rhythmically beating the carpet with the butt of a revolver. For a moment, he didn't notice them as they entered.

An armed man. This was not looking good. "Sir Sarahun?" asked Thomas.

"I'm fighting, so I'm not a monster, but human, so I'm Sir Sarahun. Who are you?"

"Rifle, PC Cavendish." Thomas decided not to mention Windy unless he was asked. "Couldn't you get the servants to do that?"

"No servants in the house today. I sent them away. Obviously."

"I see, sir. Why did you send them away?"

"To protect them from the monster. There may be a monster in the house. I have to find out." Sir Sarahun suddenly glared at Thomas. "Who are you, sir? Answer me now."

"PC Cavendish, sir. Like I said."

"Did you? If I fight you, will you fight back? Are you human or a monster?" Spittle was coming out of Sir Sarahun's mouth.

"Let's not get angry, sir."

"Of course not, but I have to know if you're human or a monster. The monsters look like people, but they're not. I find out. Do I know you? Who are you?"

"I'm PC Cavendish, sir. Put the gun down, there's a good sir."

"It's lonely having to deal with monsters. But there's a girl in the basement. She might be a monster, or she might be able to help me, then I won't be lonely."

"Girl in the basement." Thomas breathed a sigh of relief. Frank would have that covered.

"I'm sorry, I get these bad spells," Sir Sarahun said, suddenly speaking in a normal voice. "I forget things, and I get angry. Who are you?"

"PC Cavendish, sir."

"Are you a monster?" His voice was suddenly filled with rage.

"How can you tell if it's a monster?"

"When a person is attacked, they fight back. If you attack someone and they fight back, they're a person. Animals don't fight back. They freeze, like a mouse facing a snake, or they hide, or they try to escape. And an animal that looks like a person is a monster and you kill monsters."

"The girl in the basement?"

"I'm lonely, and I need a son to continue my work. But the school only ever sends me monsters. One day, I'll find the answer. Who are you?"

"PC Cavendish. So, you bring young girls here, lock them in the basement, scare them half to death, attack them, and ..." Thomas just stopped.

"You monster!" said Windy.

"Who are you? It doesn't matter. Are you a monster?" Sir Sarahun rushed towards Windy. Sir Sarahun was a good six inches taller than Windy, and heavier in build, and wasn't encumbered by a dress, and he swung the butt of the revolver at Windy. Windy swayed out of the way of the blow, and then punched like a little Jack Dempsey, left, right, left and away, and fell back into into a boxer's stance. Sir Sarahun stared, as much in surprise as pain.

"What's the matter, frozen?" said Windy, tight-lipped and angry.

Sir Sarahun looked shocked. "I froze. I didn't fight back. I'm an animal in human form. A monster. I kill monsters." He put the barrel of the revolver into his mouth, and a strange expression of peace came over his face. "It's for the best," he muttered.

Then he pulled the trigger.

*****

Peter was getting tired of being berated by Millicent. "No, I'm not going to arrest you. Grown-ups get arrested. If you're going to behave like a child, I'll punish you like a child."

"What on earth do you mean?"

"Naughty children get put over a knee and spanked."

"You wouldn't dare treat me like that."

"Go on, I would," said a voice from the crowd.

Peter had had enough of this and took a step towards her. She paused, looked at his face, and she decided discretion was the better part of valour, and beat a hasty retreat.

"Shame!"

The crowd realised that the entertainment had left, and started to disperse.

*****

Frank went down the stairs slowly and carefully, the hairs on the back of his neck rising. He could hear a low growl in the gloom. No, two. Maybe three. He could also hear a whimpering and the sound of a girl fearfully reciting the Lord's Prayer.

He put a foot on the bottom step, and he sensed rather than saw a grey shape leaping at him. Blindly, he grabbed with his left hand, and found he'd taken hold of a wolfhound. He staggered backwards, and the wolfhound was struggling to get free. He had managed to keep hold of the knife, and he plunged it into the side of the dog again and again. Stab and twist and pull out and hot blood flowing over his arm, then the hound convulsed, and then it was still.

He got to his feet. The girl was ahead of him. Two more hounds. He could hear their growls. One to the left, one to the right.

There had to be a reason why the wolfhounds hadn't attacked the girl. His eyes were slowly adjusting to the light levels. He almost wished they hadn't. At the far end of the room, a girl was in a sort of barred cage, not quite tall enough for her to stand up in. The wolfhounds were prowling about the room.

Time was running out. It had to be. He moved towards the cage. "Is cage door locked?" he asked.

"No. The man said I would be safe if I kept it shut. I'm scared."

"I here to protect you. I come towards door. Understand? When I reach door, come out, stay right close behind me. You be safe. Dogs have to get through me first, that they not do."

He hoped.

"I understand, sir. What's your name? In case, well, in case."

"Frank Barry. Truly, Francesco Barrilari, but no-one able to say it."

"Francesco. Why have you come to rescue me?"

"It my job. What your name?"

Her voice was calmer, more level. "Joy. Don't have a real last name, so they put me down as Eliot."

Step by step he walked forward over the stone-flagged floor. The floor was slippery, so he walked very cautiously. If he stumbled, the wolfhounds would be on him in a flash.

She was bearing up well. She must be terrified. "When I get to you, stand close, but not get in way of arms. Understand."

"You'll need me close, but not in your way. I understand."

He reached the door, and Joy stepped out as he had asked. She was shaking but forcing herself to stay close. As they started moving towards the stairs, the growls of the wolfhounds grew deeper and more menacing. So long as they were growling, they were safe. Growls were a threat, a warning.

The growling stopped. In the distance, there was the sound of a gunshot, muffled and strange, but unmistakable. The sound triggered the wolfhounds into action. Both sprang. He got an arm up to keep the teeth of one away from his throat and slashed at its throat. It fell away whimpering. The blow hadn't been a clean one, but it had done the job. He was turning, when the other crashed into his shoulders, knocking him to the ground. His knife went flying, and he was only able to roll in time to get his hands around the throat of the wolfhound as it strained to tear at his throat with its teeth. It was a test of strength, and they were equally matched. He tried squeezing, but his hands were slippery with blood, and he could feel his arms starting to give way. He wanted to shout to the girl to run clear, but he couldn't spare the strength.

Then the wolfhound shrieked in pain, and it weakened a little, and tried to twist, but he held it, and after a moment, it was still, dripping with blood. Joy was standing, shaking like a leaf, holding his knife, blood all over her hands, her eyes wide with near-shock.

"I stabbed it."

"You did. We get out of here."

They climbed the stairs, and he shut the door.

"I think you save my life."

She gave a weak smile. "Well, you saved mine, so that's fair."

She was still shaking. She was, he guessed, 15, maybe 16. A bit skinny, thick blonde hair, and long, sensitive fingers. She started to cry, and he put his arms round her.

"It all right. You safe now."

She looked up at him, with wide deep-blue eyes. She smiled happily, sighed and held him tightly. "I know."

*****

Thomas had been surprised at how pleased the schoolchildren were when they came back with the girl. They were back in Rifleman uniforms and they'd cleaned up, and the girl had borrowed some clothes from Beryl and Iris and looked presentable.

As the riflemen escorted Joy into the school, the children didn't know whether to applaud and cheer and wave, or to be stoic and disciplined and continue as though nothing was happening.

The riflemen received a message to go to the Headmaster's office straight away. As they were heading off, one of the teachers hurried the children along.

"It's no big deal," the teacher said. "They're Riflemen. They got the job done. What else did you expect?" The children hurried along, and as they did so, the teacher raised his hand in salute to the riflemen, then walked briskly across to them.

"Mr Charlton, formerly Corporal Charlton of the First Battalion, Rifle Brigade. Damned good work you did."

The riflemen went on their way, feeling ten feet tall, although Thomas wondered how Lady Dalkeith would bring them back to earth.

"I trust you enjoyed your break," were Lady Dalkeith's first words when they entered the office. "Obviously, I've no need to know what you did on your free time. I see you found the missing girl. That's good fortune. Mr Roberts, you are in charge of this establishment and you have a duty of care to those in this establishment. Now, charity leads to indolence. However, if you ever have a need for assistance, I am sure that it will be possible to find ways to enable you to help yourselves. I shall write a letter of introduction for you to Major Tucker, at Croydon. There will be occasions when he is able to use casual labour. You wish to say something, Rifleman Miller?"

"Yes, Ma'am. If it's casual work that's wanted, Miss Bannerman and Miss Wallace, when they're starting a new act, they often have a lot of sewing that needs doing, and they complained about how much time gets wasted preparing and repairing costumes. Girls here do sewing. Maybe something could be sorted out."

"You see, Mr Roberts? I shall leave you with a list of people you might speak to when you have such need. Now, young girl. It seems you've been removed from the school records. I shall find a suitable position for you."

Joy took a deep breath. "Beg pardon, Ma'am, I want to go with the Regiment to Persia."

"That's out of the question. Only wives will be permitted to travel and only a handful of them."

"I know, Ma'am. I want to go as Francesco's wife."

"I see. Mr Roberts, can you take Riflemen Miller, Grant, and O'Grady to continue their talk to the children." She was looking sternly at Joy and Frank, and as the others filed out, Joy took Frank's hand for reassurance. The door shut.

"Young lady, how long have you known Rifleman Barry? A few hours? It's just gratitude talking, along with a lot of romantic notions of what being a wife involves."

"Excuse me, Ma'am," Joy whispered, "but I just know that I want to be Mrs Barillari."

"Really. You have no idea what it will be like in Persia. It will be uncomfortable and hot and a very difficult place."

"I daresay, Ma'am. But I would rather be uncomfortable with Frank than live in luxury without him."

Lady Dalkeith was silent for a long time. She looked long at Joy's face, then at Frank's, then Joy's again.

"It's just gratitude speaking," she said.

"No, Ma'am. I just, well, I just know."

"I see. Rifleman Barry?"

"She was brave. She will be good wife for soldier. I would be very happy man if she my wife."

"I see. Marriage is out of the question. But before you say anything that you might regret like threatening to leave the Regiment, I want to think. Can you sew, girl?"

"Yes, Ma'am. We have to keep clothes going as long as we can, Ma'am."

"Clean?"

"Yes, Ma'am. We can't make clothes new, but we can make sure they're clean."

"I don't need explanations, just yes or no. Keep a house tidy? Run a household on a small amount of money? Cook? Keep food in good condition? Can you work hard and without constantly complaining?"

"Yes to all of those, Ma'am."

"Well, you're certainly very pretty."

"Thank you, Ma'am."

"It's an observation, not a compliment. Beauty is not important for the wife of a soldier. She's got to be able to run everything when he is away on duty and do so without causing him a moment of concern. Looks are of no use if the household is a disgrace. A soldier can rent looks."

"Yes, Ma'am."

"Very well. Here is how it will be. Marriage is, at present, out of the question. You will come in my employ as a maid. You will work hard. At the first sign of slacking or complaint, you will be back on a boat to England. Furthermore, since you will be in the Colonel's household and since you are both young and may be driven by passions, whenever you two are together, you will have a chaperone. If I ever find you together unchaperoned, you will be on a boat back to England.

"I think that what you feel is gratitude. You believe it to be genuine affection. Gratitude fades. Genuine affection doesn't. We'll know which it is after you've spent time working in an uncomfortable position. How old are you, girl?"

"Joy Eliot, Ma'am. I'm not sure, Ma'am. No-one really keeps records."

"I can't abide prevarication. You look very young. How old are you?"

Joy glanced at Frank, and then looked straight back at Lady Dalkeith. "Fifteen, Ma'am. Sixteen tomorrow."

"You look younger."

"Not enough food here, Ma'am. Everyone looks a bit young here."

"Nonetheless, you are still too young to marry. Different people are ready at different times. I will decide when you are ready. Is that understood?"

"Yes, Ma'am. Chaperoned when I'm with Frank, work hard for you, no slacking, you'll decide when I'm ready to marry Frank. Ma'am, what about?"

Lady Dalkeith raised a cold eyebrow. "Not while you are in my household. When you are married and not before. Understood?"

"Yes, Ma'am."

"As for you, Rifleman Barry, you've got something to face. The pay of a rifleman may be sufficient for a single man, but it is not sufficient to support a wife and family. It's out of the question for you to marry before you reach the rank of sergeant. When you are a sergeant, we can talk. Is that understood?"

"Yes, Ma'am. Ma'am, sergeants need to write. I read, writing is not so much."

"Ma'am, I can teach Frank his letters and writing. I helped teach the young ones here to read and write."

"Did you, indeed. I'll remember that. Rifleman Barry, when you are a sergeant, you may approach me about the matter if you still feel so inclined. Are you both clear on this?"

"Yes, Ma'am."

"I think you're both very foolish, but this way, we'll avoid bad consequences from this folly. Join the others."

"Ma'am," said Joy. "May we have a chaperone to take us to the others?"

*****

Thomas spoke to the class, explaining about the field exercise. One of the children had a raised hand. Thomas indicated that he could ask a question.

"Sir, you got back Joy, and you're going out to Persia, and you make sure that them as does important work in foreign parts is safe, and all that. Well, thing is, Sir, no-one really cares what happens to us in these schools, and the real soldiers are the ones who does all the protecting, but no-one really protects us. Only us is the people who go into the regiments to do the protecting. Them's got the police and the specials and the HSOs, and all that, protecting them, and we ain't got nobody. So why don't the soldiers just say that they'll protect us here? Only soldiers are just us growed up, so it's just protecting ourselves, and that's all them is doing."

"That's enough," said the teacher, sharply. "Terribly sorry, Rifleman. Brown's heard about these silly Socialist ideas."

"I don't know about these ideas," said Thomas to the boy. "Soldiers protect people who need protecting. No soldier is going to say to someone who needs protecting: "No, we won't do our duty because you're not the right sort of person." Joy needed rescuing. We rescued her. If she had been the daughter of a Lord, we'd have rescued her."

"But them have loads protecting them, and we ain't got no-one."

"Something I heard," said Windy. "It answers your question. It's kind of a poem.

"All good people agree,
"And all good people say,
"All nice people, like Us, are We
"And everyone else is They;
"But if you cross over the sea,
"Instead of over the way,
"You may end up by (think of it) looking on We
"As only a sort of They."

A hand shot up. "Sir, I don't understand."

"It's quite straightforward," said Thomas. "People are people. Treat them as you find them. Protect those that need protecting, whether they're a We or a They."

Another hand shot up. "Sir, I don't get how you got that from that."

Peter was inspired. "And that's something you can study. Write something about why soldiers need to protect everyone who needs protecting, and how everyone is better off when everyone contributes according to their ability. With your teacher's permission."

Another hand shot up. "Sir, who's going to read them?"

Peter had another idea, perhaps not so inspired. "Send them to Sergeant Taylor, compliments of Lady Dalkeith."

Thomas and Windy whispered their opinions on this to Peter, which summarised as: "You have just got us into trouble. Sergeant Taylor will go spare."

*****

They waited quietly in the foyer of the hotel, waiting for Lady Dalkeith and Joy to come down. They sat at a table and played bridge. Their cards were getting old and worn through use. As always, Thomas and Frank were partners. One of the hotel staff came over and told them to make sure they didn't disturb the guests with boisterous behaviour. They sat and played cards.

Windy started absent-mindedly tapping a finger against the back of his cards while he was considering his bid.

"Not do that," said Frank. "It cheating to use signal code."

"Sorry."

Eventually, Lady Dalkeith and Joy came down. Thomas glanced at Joy, and he had to remind himself that she was Frank's girl. If she hadn't been, he could have taken quite a shine to her. However, she only had eyes for Frank, at the moment.

"Come along, gentlemen. We need to make sure Miss Eliot has all the clothing that she will need. Remember, young lady, this is not a gift. It shall be coming out of your pay."

"I pay. It come from my pay," said Frank.

"Are you sure about that, Rifleman Barry? It won't be cheap, and I'm sure that your meagre pay doesn't stretch far for luxuries for yourself."

"I sure. It my responsibility."

The smile Joy gave made Thomas feel a little sad. No-one had ever smiled like that to him.

"Our pay," he said. "She's Frank's girl, so that means she's one of us and we look after our own. And that means your family as well, Windy. Don't have much spare, but it all helps."

"Is that the decision of you all? Very well. You are a very fortunate girl. We shall purchase you those items. It won't be much. Space will be in short supply. Robinson's will have everything you'll need."

"Excuse me, Ma'am," said Windy. "I know who supplies Robinson's. They buy from a sewing stall. And if I'm honest, it ain't difficult to get material and patterns. My sisters does some of their sewing."

"Can you sew from a pattern?" Lady Dalkeith asked Joy.

"Yes, Ma'am," Joy said, a little uncertainly.

"Learn," said Lady Dalkeith. "There are other things we need from the market, so you gentlemen will need to carry things. Once we are finished, you gentlemen will be at liberty for the rest of the day. I will be taking Miss Eliot to the British Museum. There are a few things there I wish to see."

"I wish come also," said Frank.

"Miss Eliot will not have free time during the trip."

Frank scowled. "As sergeant, I need know about Persia. British Museum will have information. I learn about Persia."

Lady Dalkeith permitted herself a half-smile. "You're not a sergeant."

"Yet, Ma'am" Frank said.

Shopping in a market was a new experience for Thomas. Lady Dalkeith told the riflemen what she wanted from a stall and how much she was prepared to pay for it. "You may keep the difference between that and what is actually paid."

"What if we can't get it down to that level?" Thomas asked, knowing the answer.

Lady Dalkeith just gave a look. "And remember, Rifleman Grant. These stall owners are working on small margins. I trust you understand me and that there will be no awkwardness."

They quickly discovered that Thomas was not very skilled at the negotiations. He could talk and smile and charm, especially with the women on the stalls, but getting a good price wasn't a skill he had mastered.

The others were better, although some of the quantities Lady Dalkeith wanted were surprising. A foot square piece of curtain material was odd, but simple. Eight hundred of them was much harder. Thomas asked what it was for.

"Havelocks. Attach to the cap to protect the back of the neck from the sun. Vital, and not part of official equipment. A foot square is sufficient for four. Each soldier will have one square."

Joy held onto the clothes and materials that had been bought for her. "Ma'am, I don't understand. If they're essential, why aren't they part of official equipment?"

"Because they're not necessary."

"I don't understand, Ma'am."

"The Army has determined that they may be added to field equipment at the discretion of the CO, and as such, the costs do not come from the Army."

"Thomas?" The voice was that of a lady browsing among the stalls. "I thought you were a policeman."

He turned and saw Millicent, who had seen him and was walking over. Thomas glanced desperately to Lady Dalkeith.

"Don't mind me," she said. "I'm happy for you to speak to your friend. It could prove most illuminating."

"Thomas, I called your father, but he seemed, well, confused. Anyway, he's been talking to father about some business deal or other, which has been so *horridino*. Why are you dressed like a soldier?"

"It's a disguise," Thomas said without thinking. "We're trying to catch some crooks."

"Really? How exciting. What sort of crooks?"

"White slave traders. They kidnap young ladies. We're here to catch them."

"So that's why the girl is here. Hello. I'm Millicent Steele. Thomas is an old friend of mine."

"Joy Eliot, Miss."

"An old friend of Thomas'? Fascinating. Officially, I'm Maeve Dalkeith, but I'm sure," Lady Dalkeith gave the merest pause, "Thomas can explain."

"White slavers are operating here, so Miss Eliot is the bait, and she's terribly brave about it. Daughter of the inspector, of course. And Detective Sergeant Taylor here is acting as the madame offering the sale. The others are in disguise as Riflemen."

"But you look like a soldier, not a rifleman."

"Riflemen are soldiers, Millicent."

"What happened to that other girl. Not as pretty as you, Miss Eliot. From yesterday."

"Ah. Wendy Miller. Yes. She's with another group further east. It's a big operation."

"I was sure I saw someone who looked just like her, but a man in a soldier's uniform."

"Her brother. Um, Ma'am, um."

"This seems like a very jolly adventure. Why did you call Detective Sergeant Taylor Ma'am?" Millicent sounded intrigued.

"Because she's in disguise. He's in disguise. That's the trick of being undercover. You have to remember that you're pretending to be someone else. Um, is there anything I should get, Ma'am."

"It seems to me you need a spade, to dig yourself out of the hole you keep stepping into." Lady Dalkeith relented. "But I think it wise to remove a civilian from the line of fire. We wouldn't want the white slavers to target the wrong lady, would we. You had best escort Miss Steele to a safe place."

As Thomas escorted Millicent from the market, he tried not to think how much trouble he was in. He wasn't really listening to her prattle on.

"Which hotel are you staying at?" he asked.

"The Carlton, obviously. What do you think, then?"

"I think you don't need me to tell you. Isn't that what Votes for Women is about? Women thinking for themselves, not just taking a man's word for it."

"Thank you. I knew you'd understand. Daddy and your father are so, well, they don't understand. And I can't see why your father got confused. He insisted that I must have been mistaken when I said I spoke to you." She giggled. "It must be a bit of a lark for you, pretending to be one of the servants. It's all a bit looking glass."

"How do you mean?" Thomas was starting to have a bad feeling about this.

"Well, you always used to seduce the servants all over the place."

"I did not. One or two, maybe, but that was, just something that happened."

"One or two? There was Poppy, and Anne, Elizabeth, Emily, Marie when you had that row with your father and stayed over at Daddy's house. Mary, Sarah, Susan, Georgina,"

"I didn't seduce Georgina. Who's Georgina?"

"Worked in the stables. Fair hair, strong arms."

"Oh yes, right. That wasn't, well, *I* didn't seduce *her*. Anyway, even if it's true, which it isn't, how do you know all this?"

"I told you. Daddy and your father are trying to get me married off and I want a bit of fun first, and ever since you nearly gave me flying lessons, I was rather looking forward to you seducing me, but you were always more interested in serving girls."

"I'm afraid I can't," Thomas said desperately. "I've got to get back on duty."

"Pfah. The Detective Sergeant, and mind you, he looked nothing like a woman, said that you were to see me safe. So that means you've got to escort me into my room, and I'm scared there might be white slavers in it."

Thomas gave the first excuse that came into his head. "I'm married."

"What? When? Who to?"

"Married. Last week. To a nurse, red hair, nice smile, Nurse Charrington. She was Nurse Charrington. She's Mrs O'G, Mrs Cavendish, Nurse Cavendish now. And I believe in the sanctity of marriage, so here's your hotel and goodbye."

As he headed back at a half-run, Thomas wondered if he should have told her not to tell father.

*****

Thomas couldn't find the others at the market. Lady Dalkeith had said that they were on liberty for the rest of the day. Frank, Joy, and Lady Dalkeith were going to the British Museum, and there was no way Thomas intended to go there. He had no idea what Peter and Windy were going to do. That meant that he was on his own for the rest of the day.

He went to Tower Bridge to watch the river. He didn't have any money. Correction, he had two shillings and a penny. With care, that would but a cheap meal and a pint of beer.

It felt strange to be in a position to have the time to spend money, but not have any money to spend. If he'd had any sense, he would have accepted Millicent's offer, and then they could have gone out on the town, and her father was very well off, so payment wouldn't have been a problem.

He couldn't work out why he hadn't accepted the offer. Millicent was pretty, and what with training and being in barracks, he hadn't had female companionship for some time.

He stared at the brown water of the river, ignoring the smell of oil and dirt and coal dust. It was probably too late to go back to Millicent's hotel and have his way with her. Even if it wasn't, he found that he didn't particularly want to.

She wouldn't smile at him the way Joy smiled at Frank. No-one had ever smiled like that at him, and he was jealous. Joy wouldn't smile like that for him, probably, but surely someone would.

That was another thing. Why did Joy smile for Frank?

He shook his head. He'd never understand women.

There was another thought nagging at him. Why was his father involved in arranging a marriage for Millicent? He'd always spoken with disdain about the family. Never invited them over. What was going on?

Father had kept to his promise to disown and disinherit him if he left. Father always kept his promises, whatever the cost. It had cost him quite a lot over the years. He now had a large house with no-one but him and the servants, and he disapproved of fraternising with servants.

"They work for you. They're not your friends."

What would happen to the place if father died?

And that reminded him. Sir Sarahun didn't have a family, as far as he knew, and he was now dead. According to a newspaper, he died when the gun he was cleaning accidentally discharged. Now there would be just the servants there. Maybe looking would give him an idea what might happen should anything happen to father.

*****

The British Museum was big, Frank thought. The entrance doors were big enough for giants. Why did they make the doors so big? And what was the point of fiddly bits of stonework all over the place with letters spelling out words that weren't actually words.

Inside there were huge rooms filled with carefully displayed old rubbish. What was the point of half of a rusty sword without a hilt? There was a whole display case of them.

"We came to learn about the Persians, Ma'am," said Joy.

"No, Joy. Rifleman Barry came to learn about the Persians. I came to talk to someone here. About Persia, as it happens." Lady Dalkeith thought for a moment. "I had intended for you to be with me, but I think Rifleman Barry would benefit if you were there to help him read the descriptions alongside the exhibits. You may go with him to do this. I expect the two of you to behave yourselves appropriately, on your words of honour."

"Ma'am, you say we always need chaperone."

"Rifleman Barry, your behaviour has been such that in a public place, you have earned a short period of privacy. Honourable behaviour. Understood?"

"Yes, Ma'am. Thank you, Ma'am."

It was hard. Frank received many hard stares from other people viewing the exhibits. He wasn't sure if he should let his fingers touch Joy's when he held doors open for her.

"They may think the Uniform of Honour is a joke," said Joy, "but you are a man of honour and a hero, and I think you are the best man in the world."

They reached the Persian exhibits, and Frank was shocked when he saw one of the statues, which was of a man laying down on a couch; the man was not wearing any clothes. No-one seemed bothered by this. Then he was even more shocked on seeing a statue of a woman standing reaching up for something, and she wasn't wearing any clothes either.

"It's all right," whispered Joy. "It's art."

"But," Frank started, and realised he didn't know what to say, and there were other women, and they were looking at the statues.

"And Persepolis," said Joy. "Do you think we'll be near there?"

"Where Persepolis."

"I learned him at school. Is it not passing brave to be a king, and ride in triumph through Persepolis."

"I not a king."

"Yes, you are. You're my king."

"Excuse me, Tommy, Miss," said a man with a sketch pad. Tall man with a rather grubby jacket, a broad smile, and calculating eyes. "May I take a sketch of you two while we talk? We don't often see a Tommy in here."

"I here."

"We're going to Persia soon, so we came to learn more about it."

"You're his wife?"

"Soon," Joy said happily.

"Aren't you scared about going to Persia? Wouldn't you rather stay home in England?" The man was sketching as he asked the questions.

"It'll be hard work and uncomfortable and possibly dangerous, but I'll be with my Frank. I would rather be uncomfortable with him than living in luxury without him. Any wife would."

The man didn't seem entirely convinced that all wives would choose their husband over luxury, but he didn't say that. "Why?"

"Because I love my Frank."

"Aren't you scared?"

"Of course I'm scared. But I'm English. My place is with my husband."

"And you, Tommy. Are you happy for your wife to go into danger?"

"Have you tried talking your wife out of doing something she determined to do? It not possible."

"What do you think about the current situation in Persia?"

"It not for me to say. I just a Rifleman."

"Surely you're worried about how complicated the situation is out there?"

"For Rifleman, it simple. Do duty, behave with honour and courage."

"Come, are honour and courage that important in this day and age?"

"They most important things. Honour tell us what right thing to do is. Courage give strength to do it. All else depend on honour and courage."

"Thank you, Tommy, Miss," the man said, finishing the sketch. "May I ask your names?"

"Rifleman Frank Barry, and I'm Miss Joy Eliot, engaged to the most wonderful man in the world."

"Who you?" Frank asked. He was suspicious.

"James Lancaster, Daily Herald, published every Saturday. We're doing a piece on the scandal of the Persian situation, and how our incompetence at every level is making a bad situation worse. Courage and Honour. That's good."

*****

Peter suggested going to see Windy's family. Windy explained that his family were Pacifists and wouldn't let a soldier into the house.

"But you send all your money home. They're happy to take your money, but not to see you?"

"They don't like what I'm doing, but they know I had no choice. They would see me, but no other soldier."

"That's wrong."

"Oh, they know I'm going to Hell for what I'm doing, but that I'm doing it for them."

Peter didn't push the point, but he thought Windy wasn't telling the truth. Something odd was going on.

Windy sighed with relief. Peter had accepted the story. He wanted to see his family, but he couldn't if Peter was there. "Let's go to see the football. Tottenham are playing Newcastle. You can buy me a pint for every goal Tottenham score, and I'll buy you one for every goal Newcastle score."

*****

"I don't think you'll be able to manage all those," said Peter. "I may as well sign the Pledge. Four to nothing. It's a disgrace."

"Bert Bliss was good, wasn't he?"

*****

Thomas arrived at Sir Sarahun's house. There were about half a dozen policemen trying to keep order outside the place, and a small crowd at the gate. The crowd seemed to be angry, and the police seemed to be struggling to keep them from bursting into the place.

Thomas thought about leaving, but someone saw him and pointed at him. "They're sending the Army."

For some reason, this caused many in the crowd to disperse, easing the pressure on the police. Confused, Thomas walked towards the police.

"What's going on?" he asked.

The policeman in charge looked a bit puzzled. "Are you an officer, Sir? Only you're wearing a Ranker's uniform."

"Rifle Brigade," said Thomas. "Never a good idea to give enemy an easy target. That's why we have black buttons." It wasn't a lie, exactly.

"Very good, Sir. They were, well, they'd heard Sir Sarahun had died, and, well, they had funny ideas."

"Why wasn't he Sir Albert?"

"Some sort of foreigner, Sir. That's what they say, anyway."

"Servants?"

"They've refused to come in until the place is made safe."

"Made safe?"

"They won't say, Sir."

"I see. It's lucky I came along. Look, your patch and all that, but scouting out for trouble, that's what we're trained for. How would it be if I took a quick look around inside, and then come back and tell you what I find. You need your boys out here, and if I'm quick, you'll impress your bosses with how thoroughly you scouted it out." Thomas had a plan.

"I don't know, Sir. I'm not supposed to let anyone in. But I suppose it can't do any harm, Sir. Don't be long, or I'll have to send someone in, and that'll cause problems."

"I understand. Don't worry, I'll not be long. Just a quick scout out."

"Very good, Sir. You haven't told me your name."

"Haven't I? Call me Nicholas. Lieutenant Nicholas Furley-Smith."

"Be quick, Sir."

Thomas was pleased with himself. He hadn't actually told a lie.

*****

The important thing was that he had a chance to look around the house on his own. There had been all sorts of things lying around, and this was likely to be his last chance for adventure before going out to Persia. He'd also wondered how difficult it would be.

He'd remembered that there was a large, colourful Gladstone bag in Sir Sarahun's bedroom, ideal for carriage. Paintings were out of the question, impossible to transport.

The police were conveniently keeping looters out, leaving him with the run of the place. This was going to be good practise for operating independently. There was a slight risk involved, so he had to be on his guard, but if the worst came to the worst, he'd just suffer an embarrassment.

Upstairs, and collect the bag. Nice and quiet. The drapes around the bed were good quality, and would be good for wrapping breakables in. Downstairs to the library, and half a dozen books. The trip to Persia would be long and railway novels would get monotonous. Make sure a couple of the books are suitable for appeasing authority.

Then to the basement. Two sets of stairs. He thought he heard some scratching. Probably rats.

Down the first set of stairs. Cool here, and success. It was the wine cellar. He needed to be quick. He could only fit maybe eight bottles in the bag at most. Two bottles of whisky were on a table. Into the bag and wrap the drape around them. If they don't clink, they won't break. He wished that he knew more about wine. Father had always dealt with that. Still, you don't store bad wine in a cellar, so any half dozen would do. He thought he heard something scratching inside the walls. Time to get out of here, check the other basement, and then leave.

He opened the door to the other basement, and there was a strong smell of something unpleasant. He stepped carefully onto the first step and peered down into the gloom. He wasn't sure about this at all and paused. As he paused, he felt something push him in the back, and he started to slip and slide down the stairs. He grabbed hold of something to stop himself. Unfortunately, it was a foot, and all he succeeded in doing was drag his assailant down the steps with him.

They landed together in a heap at the bottom. His assailant tried to get up but was trapped underneath him.

"What's this all about?" Thomas asked. Then he realised his assailant was a girl, wearing a maid's uniform. "What are you doing here?"

"Don't hurt me, sir, not like that bad man."

"Don't be silly. I don't hurt girls. What's your name? What are you doing here?"

The girl was young, still a teenager, with a thin face and large, dark brown eyes. She looked scared. Slim, almost skinny.

"Diana, sir. My name's Diana. Please don't hurt me like that other man."

"Don't be silly, I won't hurt you. Why are you here?"

"I was out walking, sir, when someone grabs me and brings me here. The gentleman here, he hurts me, and then said he'd leave me for the dogs, but I was able to climb up and get away from them, and there was a small hole in the wall where I could hide, and I've been stuck here and stealing food from the dogs when they was fed and I'm scared."

"You're safe now. Come on, let's get you out of here." He helped her up, and she looked around warily.

"You're not going to hurt me?"

"Of course not. Come on, let's get you out of here." He picked up the bag and led the way out the back of the house.

"Where are we going?" she asked.

"I just need to drop something off at the back gate," Thomas said, holding her arm for reassurance. She clung close to him, looking around anxiously. She didn't ask why he was dropping the bag off here, which Thomas was grateful for, because he couldn't think of a good explanation. Then it was just a matter of returning to the house and heading to the front gate.

"I see you caught one, Lieutenant," said the policeman. "There are always ghouls who'll try and steal from the dead."

"It's not like that. Diana was kidnapped and held prisoner by, someone from the household."

"I see, sir. Well done, Lieutenant."

A woman was with the other policeman, and she spoke. "Lieutenant?" Thomas' heart sank. It was Millicent.

"Yes, Ma'am. This is Lieutenant Furley-Smith, of the Rifle Brigade," said the policeman.

"Millicent, what are you doing here?" Thomas looked around desperately for an escape route.

"I followed you, silly. You're using so many names I'm getting confused and I'm very curious."

"Different names, sir?" asked the policeman.

Thomas took the policeman slightly to one side. "It's like this, constable. I'm, well, I'm a married man. Sometimes it makes life easier if I don't use my real name. I'm sure you understand."

The policeman stiffened. "I'm afraid I do understand, sir. You might want to consider the sanctity of the Marriage Oath, sir, for the betterment of your soul. Nonetheless, you did rescue the girl."

"Exactly where was she hiding?" Millicent asked.

Thomas and Diana retold the story. Millicent didn't look impressed.

"Men," she snorted. "So, you went walking in a maid uniform? Any maid of mine that did that would be looking for a new job. Your shoes look awfully neat and unscratched for someone who has gone through such an ordeal. You hid inside the gap in the wall? And there's not a trace of brick dust on your uniform. Remarkable. No brick dust in your hair. And you look remarkably well fed for someone who's been living off dog food for some days."

"I *thought* you were one of them thieving ghouls," said the policeman, and the girl took to her heels with the policeman in hot pursuit.

Once the policeman had left, Millicent turned to Thomas. "Lieutenant Furley-Smith, Rifleman O'Grady, Constable Cavendish? You're an army all by yourself."

"That was well observed, Millicent. If you'll excuse me, I have some work to do." Thomas started to walk to the back gate to collect the bag. Millicent walked with him.

"Thomas Cavendish. I have spoken with my father, and he has said that he is determined that I should be married. I want some fun before I get married, and if you don't oblige me in that, I shall be forced to mention to a policeman how many different names you're wearing."

"But I'm married."

"And your wife's name is? Her first name."

"Um, Agatha."

"Umagatha. Unusual name.

Thomas picked up the bag. "Millicent, truthfully, I'm not married, but there is a girl I admire greatly. Nurse Charrington. I don't know her well enough to know her first name, but, well, this feels different"

Millicent looked at him for a moment. "Do you know, I think you're actually telling the truth. Is Thomas really smitten by a girl after all this? Very well, we can have fun without flying lessons. And if I have a lot of fun, I'll tell your father that I was mistaken and it wasn't you I saw."

"My father?"

"Yes, he's coming down tomorrow with Father. Now, I fancy dinner at the Café de Paris. They've got that hot band playing there, with some dancing that everyone says is simply immoral. Well, it would be. Jamaican musicians, can you believe it."

"My bag," said Thomas.

"We'll put it in my hotel room. It'll be safe there, and you can pick it up after we've had an evening out."

When they were dropping the bag off in her hotel room, Millicent shut the door. "Last chance," she said. "Admit it, you're tempted."

Thomas had to admit he was very tempted. All he could think of was Oscar Wilde's advice about how to get rid of temptation, and he didn't think that was very helpful. "The only way to get rid of temptation was to give in to it." It had been a long time.

*****

Windy really couldn't hold his drink, Peter thought. Four pints, and he'd gone past merry and into not quite coherent. Time to get him back to the room and into his bed.

"I'm not really a Rifleman, you know," Windy muttered. "You're my best friend. I can tell you I'm not a real Rifleman."

"Come on," Peter said, helping Windy to his feet and supporting him as they started to weave their unsteady way from the pub. Despite the hard work of recruit training, and subsequent training, Windy still seemed to have a bit of chubbiness here and there. That's boys for you. Still getting rid of puppy fat.

*****

Dinner and dancing wouldn't be too bad. It might even be quite fun. Millicent was quite pretty, in a gullible, brainless sort of way.

"Why's my father involved in these talks about getting you married off?" he asked.

"Isn't that obvious? This is the last chance for you to give me flying lessons to build up an appetite for dinner." She ran a hand across his shoulders, and he was very tempted. Very, very tempted. Was Oscar Wilde right?

The restaurant was noisy and busy. The Jamaican Jazz Band was really jolly good, and he'd only been able to get in by dint of not wearing his uniform. He really shouldn't, but the restaurant would never allow a soldier across its threshold. Lots of customers, all of them well-dressed and young and boisterous.

Millicent thought it was all a bit of an adventure, and joked about all the names Thomas had been using. She also quizzed him about Nurse Charrington, thinking it a great joke that he seemed to have been smitten.

The band was enthusiastic and active, although their techniques were somewhat unorthodox. Mind you, Thomas could see what the newspapers meant when they described jazz music as lascivious jungle rhythms. He was quite enjoying it.

"Are they some of your friends?" Millicent asked, glancing towards some soldiers at a table. Soldiers in green jackets. Officers. Thomas' heart sank. One of them was Lieutenant Furley-Smith.

His heart sank even further when he saw that Lieutenant Furley-Smith had recognised him. Thomas guided Millicent back to their table, hoping against hope that the Lieutenant was having too good a time to come over.

His hopes were dashed.

"A delight to make your acquaintance, Miss. Lieutenant Nicholas Furley-Smith, at your service. I apologise for my forwardness, but I thought your companion looked like a soldier in the Regiment."

"But it's not forward at all, Lieutenant Furley-Smith. We've already been introduced."

"We have? I'm absolutely certain I would remember such a delightful encounter."

"Lieutenant Furley-Smith, wasn't it, Thomas?"

Lieutenant Furley-Smith glanced at Thomas, then turned his attention back to Millicent. "I think I understand. Since we've been introduced, there can be no awkwardness about my inviting you to dance."

From that point on, Millicent and Lieutenant Furley-Smith spent a lot of time dancing and laughing and flirting. Thomas wanted to quietly leave, but his bag was in Millicent's hotel room. Lady Dalkeith expected him back by midnight, and it was already gone eleven, and they were still dancing energetically, something called the Turkey Trot, which looked ridiculous. They came back for some food, and Thomas asked Millicent about the bag.

"Oh, you'll be able to pick it up in the morning."

"If you don't mind, Bubbles, I would like a quick word with this young scoundrel."

Millicent went back to the dance floor and Lieutenant Furley-Smith's expression turned instantly to a stern one, traced with anger.

"You're not in uniform. You're in a place that specifically bars you. You've been using false names. You've pretended to be an officer. Unless I'm very much mistaken, that bag contains ill-gotten loot. Do you have the first idea just how much trouble you're in?"

"Sorry, Sir."

"You see, O'Grady, the thing about losing your past is that you actually have to leave it behind you. Now you've given me a big problem."

"Sorry, Sir."

"Luckily for you, the other officers haven't recognised you. Do you know how much trouble you would be in if I take official notice of this?"

"No, Sir."

"The looting alone is twenty ten. Pretending to be an officer, an additional ten five."

"Sir?"

"Twenty ten. Twenty lashes in front of the company, ten years hard labour. That's just for the looting." He paused to let that sink in. "However, we're going to Persia. John, that's Lieutenant Hawkins, says that you have the makings of a good Rifleman, and I would rather have you doing your duty there than breaking rocks on some God-forsaken moor. So, this is what's going to happen. Officially, I haven't recognised you. As far as I am aware, you're just some chap whose girl I'm stealing for the night. That deals with everything except the looting. Regulations distinguish between foraging, which is for the Regiment, and looting, which is for personal gain. You were foraging. Everything gets distributed to the Regiment. And not, mark you, to your comrades. If you keep so much as a button, you'll be breaking rocks for the next twenty years. Understood? Good. I'm going to keep a close eye on you in future, and you're not getting off scot-free. Out in Persia, we'll be using mules a lot. We've acquired some of the old screw-guns, which could be useful. You've just volunteered to learn how to handle mules, and the first part of that is making sure our current stables are clean, in your free time because you are as keen as mustard. And brush down the horses.

Unfortunately, we've only a few horses. Still, I'm sure we can add to them somehow. Since I'm confident your three comrades were involved in your dubious activities, they will also be required to assist you. You can give them the glad tidings. We'll escort Bubbles back to her hotel, you collect your damn bag, and then make yourself scarce. She's mine for the night. Understand?"

"Yes, Sir. Sorry, Sir."

Millicent returned, and the Lieutenant instantly switched to the young, frivolous charmer that he had been, his stern expression just a memory.

*****

Frank was nervous, but he had to explain. "Ma'am, I think I make mistake. I talk to man, but he from newspaper."

"Did you say anything you shouldn't have done?"

"Ma'am, I not *know* anything I shouldn't."

"What, exactly, did you tell them?"

Between them, Frank and Joy were able to recreate most of the conversation.

"That seems harmless enough. However, newspapers twist words. The Daily Herald, you say. That comes out on a Saturday, so we have a week. If we try to get them to kill the story, that will just make things worse. They are the only people who can stop the story, and the only reason they'd do that is if the story was of no value. They hate the Government, the Army, and pretty much everything. You want to be a Sergeant. What do we do?"

Frank thought long and hard. "They want story," he said, slowly.

"Good. Go on."

"If it not story, if it not news, they not interested."

"Very good. Go on."

"Give them better story? No, that just make things worse."

Joy started to speak, but Lady Dalkeith shook her head. "He wants to be a Sergeant. He needs to be able to think this out for himself."

"It a story because it is news. If it not news, then it not a story." Frank paused, uncertain "If story already told, it is no longer news. We tell story again to newspaper that print before Saturday. Friendly newspaper."

"Excellent. You really are a sneaky, conniving devil. That's a good thing for a Sergeant. It's time for dinner. Let's see if the Editor of the Telegraph has someone available."

*****

The journey back had been uneventful. Joy had stared out of the window at the countryside, amazed at all the green, and constantly asking Frank what the things she could see were. Lady Dalkeith had seen Thomas' bag, but refrained from comment.

Windy was suffering from a hangover, holding his head in his hands and looking pale. Peter alternately made fun of him and stopped the others from making fun.

"We've all got to learn how to handle drink," he said.

The carriage was quiet on the journey back. Lady Dalkeith slept; Windy suffered in a corner; Thomas worried how he was going to tell the others about their punishment; Joy and Frank were too busy watching the countryside and smiling at each other; Peter was saying nothing because it was his turn to read the railway novel.

The camp was quiet when they returned.

"I need go see Sergeant Taylor," said Frank.

"I need to see some people," Thomas muttered. "Sergeant Taylor first of all."

"Yes, I rather think you have a lot to get sorted, Rifleman O'Grady. Young lady, you will start your duties now. Your first task will be to check our quarters and ensure that everything is as it should be and familiarise yourself with where everything is and how it is stored. It is imperative that you fold clothes properly, otherwise creases will be in the wrong place. You will also familiarise yourself with the layout of the camp, and who everyone is, especially people you may have dealings with in the course of your duties. By this time tomorrow, I will expect you to know all that basic information."

"Yes, Ma'am. Thank you, Ma'am."

"Do your work to my standards. No slacking. You have until we leave for Persia to prove yourself."

*****

Thomas went to see Sergeant Taylor ahead of Frank. "Sergeant Taylor, while I was in London, I met someone I knew from when I was a civilian."

He paused and checked what he had said. That was true.

"They were very kind to me." That was also true. "When I left, they gave me this bag, which included these two bottles of spirits."

That was technically true.

"I know that Riflemen aren't allowed to store spirits and have to drink it when issued. I can't keep these bottles, so I wish to give them to you for the Sergeants' Mess.

Sergeant Taylor was instantly suspicious. "Why?"

Thomas smiled ruefully. "If I tried to keep them, you'd find them and confiscate them. Then you'd have them and I would be in your bad books. This way, you have them, but I'm in your good books."

"That's your story, is it? Well, you've dug yourself out of a hole. I believe you and your bag have other people to see. Dismissed."

*****

Sergeant Taylor had barely looked at the labels on the bottles when Rifleman Barry asked to speak with him.

"I wish become Sergeant."

"That's ambitious. Why?"

Frank stood straight and stared at the wall over Sergeant Taylor's shoulder. "Lady Dalkeith has maid. I wish to marry maid. Lady Dalkeith say I may only ask when I am Sergeant. I wish to become Sergeant."

"Lad, we don't make people sergeant just so they can have a maid."

"I know. If I bad Sergeant, I not stay sergeant for long. That would make Lady Dalkeith unhappy, maybe end marriage. I wish become good sergeant. I like for you tell me how I become good sergeant."

"Pretty, is she?"

"Very. She also brave and make good soldier's wife. She show courage in danger."

Sergeant Taylor nodded thoughtfully. "Get one thing straight, Rifleman. Promotions only come by merit. If you can do the job of sergeant, we'll eventually make you a sergeant. If you can't do the job, we won't. Sit down." He gestured to a chair at the side of a desk covered with a stack of papers. The papers looked like letters.

"You want to be a good sergeant. Why come to me? I don't promote people to sergeants."

"Before I get to be sergeant, I need to be good to be sergeant. I want you teach me how to be good sergeant for when I get made sergeant."

"Being a Sergeant is all about anatomy, lad."

"I not understand."

"You need eyes in the back of your head. You need to keep track of what everyone is up to, where they are and what they're doing. You need a thick skin, because riflemen don't like you stopping their games and making sure they're doing what they should, and they'll have hard names for you when you're doing your job, and your officer will have hard words for you if the men aren't exactly how he wants them. Your officer will also worry at you in private, and will take out his worries on you, and you got to keep your officer happy because he's got to lead them.

"You need an elephant's memory, and you've got to know every trick in the book, because they'll try it on, and you've got to let them know they can't get one past you. You've got to be perfect. When you was in training, who got you up in the morning? It was me, and I was already dressed and spotless for the day when I did so.

And I was spotless when I gives you lights out. You got to be always, always spotless and ready for anything.

"You have to know everything. Is a rifle dirty? Who's had bad news from their family? What's the state of the latrines? Which soldiers can be trusted to get the job done, and which can be trusted to gets into trouble? Which soldiers aren't eating right, and who's likely to get cholera? When do you stick by Regulations and when do you turn a blind eye? How do you get what you need for the job without worrying your officer with details? Where do you get eggs and rum and shovels and horse food and any blessed thing that will be needed? How do you get the job done when the job's impossible?

"Do you still want to be a Sergeant? Lot easier being a rifleman. Don't have to think or take any responsibility."

"I want to be Sergeant. More now, I think."

"Show me I can trust you with the first step. I've got these to finish."

"What these, Sergeant?"

"Letters from a State School. I've got to write thank you letters. It's expected."

"I need improve my writing. I can write letters for you."

"It's your lucky day. Here you go," Sergeant Taylor said, handing over the pile. "Read each one, write a short reply, thanking them for the letter. Answer any questions, write something that proves you've read it. Bring them to me in the morning. How are you going to get them written? You're down as not a scholar."

"Lady Dalkeith maid promise to teach me write better."

*****

Next stop was Lieutenant Hawkins. Thomas wondered if he should stick to the same story that he had told Sergeant Taylor, or come up with an explanation designed for him. He was quite enjoying coming up with explanations.

"Come," snapped Lieutenant Hawkins. Thomas entered and his heart sank. Lieutenant Furley-Smith was there, as well as one of the Lieutenants from the dragoons. He'd best keep his story the same.

"And that's how I came by these six bottles of wine, Sir. Thought you might like them for the Officers' Mess."

"So how much trouble are you in, O'Grady?" Lieutenant Hawkins asked.

"I'd guess about six bottles of wine worth of trouble," the dragoon Lieutenant said. Thomas thought he recognised him. Yes, he did. The Lieutenant from that dragoon patrol they ambushed. The Lieutenant seemed to recognise him as well. Thomas wondered why he was here, but knew that he wouldn't be told.

"O'Grady, I gather from Sergeant Taylor that you have volunteered to assist with mule training. Lieutenant Campbell is going to be in charge of that side of things."

"We've already met," said Lieutenant Campbell. "On the exercise. Don't worry, I won't hold it against you, O'Grady."

Thomas did his best to keep his face expressionless. He knew what that meant. It meant that he did bear a grudge. Still, at least it would only last until they left for Persia.

"He'll be looking after our mule section when we're out in Persia," Lieutenant Hawkins added. "He's on secondment to us as the equine expert. You'll probably see a lot of him."

Could today get any worse? Then he remembered what he had to do next.

"Sir, request permission to speak with Colonel Dalkeith."

"Your funeral," said Lieutenant Hawkins. "What's it about?"

"Got something from London for him, Sir."

"Very well. Requestmen tomorrow morning. He'll be in a bad mood."

*****

Lady Dalkeith watched Joy as she unpacked the bags from the trip. It was important to ensure that good habits were established straight away. Clothes to be folded preparatory to being washed; important not to let creases start to appear. Make the preparations for cleaning before starting cleaning, and make sure that all the necessities to produce tea on demand were to hand.

She gave a grudging nod of approval as Joy seemed to know the basics.

"I understand that you think that you are in love with Rifleman Barry."

"I do love him, Ma'am. Very much."

Lady Dalkeith snorted. "Firstly, you barely know him. What you feel is based on what you imagine he is. You have no idea if that's what he's like. Secondly, love isn't tested in good times. It's easy to feel well-disposed to someone when things are going well and you agree on everything. Love is tested when you are tired and hungry and struggling with everything, when you're not well, and your husband expects his dinner, and the house kept tidy, when you're arguing about something and he won't listen to you. That's when you'll know if it's love or just convenience."

"Ma'am," said Joy, greatly daring. "Have you had arguments with Colonel Dalkeith?"

"We've been married for 35 years."

"Yes, but have you had arguments, beg pardon, Ma'am?"

"I gave you an answer."

"I don't understand, Ma'am."

"When you have been married for 35 years, you will."

*****

There was an unusual atmosphere about morning parade. Normally it was a matter of standing still and dozing to attention. Six months ago, Thomas wouldn't have believed it was possible to doze while standing upright, marching on command, and with eyes open. Now it was simply second nature.

Today was different. Colonel Dalkeith was there and preparing to speak to the Regiment. This was unusual and, as a result, the riflemen were actually awake.

"I have received orders concerning our next deployment. As these orders have been rated confidential, everyone is, from this moment, confined to barracks until we depart, in three days. Wives are being contacted, and we have been allocated sufficient space for 1 in 5 to accompany the Regiment. If requests to accompany the

Regiment exceed the spaces available, the usual lottery will determine the successful applicants.

"To avoid speculation, I can tell you we will be going to Persia. You have three days to get your affairs into order.

"I will see Company commanders in my office after parade.

"Much of our time in Persia will be spent working with the Persian Army. We will be showing them how to do things properly. Most of you will be in your normal companies, and will continue in that way, setting an example for the Persians to aspire to.

"Lieutenant Hawkins, your platoon is most newly trained, and the training should be fresh for your men. You will be involved in passing on lessons directly to Persian troops. When we arrive in Persia, your platoon will be expanded to company size with Persian volunteers.

"Company sergeants, take command of your companies. Company commanders, briefing."

Sergeant Taylor marched to the front of the platoon, then along the front row, shaking his head sadly.

"As the Colonel said, the platoon will expand, from 32 to 128. The bulk will be wogs and dagos, so we don't expect very much from any of them. You'll be doing most of the work. However, it means we will need extra non-coms. Riflemen Grant, Miller, O'Grady, front and centre. You have been selected from a host of volunteers to be Lance Corporals. You will do the job to my satisfaction, or you will find yourselves demoted so far you'll have to salute wog Riflemen Recruits. Is that clear? Back to your places. Rifleman Barry, front and centre. I need a Corporal what understands how dagoes think and you're the closest we've got, so you are hereby promoted to Corporal. Don't mess it up."

He leaned forward to hand the stripes to Frank, and whispered: "Here's your chance, lad. Good luck."

*****

Frank knew that Joy would be busy. Lady Dalkeith would see to that. He ought to wait. But he wanted to see Joy's smile when he showed her the stripes. He was half-way to the house, when he slowed his pace to think. He had to start thinking like a sergeant.

Be one step ahead. That's what he had to do. Lady Dalkeith would be annoyed if he tried to disturb Joy, and that would get Joy into trouble. Therefore, he had to get Lady Dalkeith's approval first.

Lady Dalkeith wouldn't give approval unless there was a good reason to give approval. She probably wouldn't consider wanting to give Joy the news as soon as possible as a good reason. The Regiment was getting ready to go to Persia. That will involve a lot of preparations, and Sergeant Taylor said that Sergeants were the backbone of the Regiment.

That meant that he would have a lot of work to do. That meant that he could honestly say he didn't know what time he would finish. Would that be enough? He had to think like a sergeant. No, it wouldn't be enough. Lady Dalkeith would say that the sooner he started the work, the sooner he would be finished.

He had to think of something that meant he needed to speak with Joy sooner rather than later. He had a thought, smiled and straightened his shoulders.

*****

He wasn't listening, honestly. He was waiting outside while the officers were being briefed. He was just waiting for Requestmen, when he could give the Colonel the book. He stood at ease with his head near the window. It was in the shade, and it just so happened that he could hear what was being said if he leaned a bit.

"That's the official situation, and how our Lords and Masters see the facts on the ground." It was the Colonel's voice. "There's a detachment of the Royal Navy Airships who will support us, but who are not in our command chain. In charge of the Navy detachment is Commander Prince Digvijaysihnji. The word is that the Navy don't quite know what to do with him and sent him there where he's out of the way. There are no Royal Marines in the Naval detachment, but there are some Sikhs. I'm not sure I understand that, but that the Navy for you. Remind your sergeants we need to be on good terms with the Navy.

"We will be supporting the Persian Army. Officially, it's large, well-equipped, well-trained, and the officers are Emperor Qajar's finest. Officially, it is a powerful force, and our task is to provide an elite component and an example for them. Unofficially, word is that the officers are more interested in playing politics and being seen around Court rather than being deployed on the borders. Officially, we'll be supporting them. Unofficially, we'll be doing all the work and they'll be taking all the credit.

"Trouble spots. Afghanistan to the north east. Because the Persian Army stays at home, the Afghan tribes believe they can raid the border villages with impunity. Arab nomads in the west of the country believe they can raid border villages with impunity. This is complicated by the fact that they are causing problems for the Turks, and our Government views the Turks having this trouble is a good thing. However, our problem will be that when the Ottoman Army retaliates, it isn't very discriminating in who they retaliate against. We will be required to prevent such retaliation taking place on Persian territory, and we are not to upset anyone while doing this.

"In the north east, the Turks have been conducting operations against internal groups, many of whom have decamped into Persia. The Persians don't want an influx of outsiders. Officially, these camps are under Persian law. Unofficially, bandits are encouraged to target them and drive them out, conveniently meaning that the bandits are not targeting Persians.

"To the north, our Russian allies do not recognise Persian control of parts of that land, and are trying to settle it with their own people in abandoned villages. Obviously, these settlers are private individuals who have nothing to do with the Russians if they get ousted, and if they remain, they ask for Russian protection. We are instructed not to upset our Russian allies, and also to maintain the integrity of Persian rule there.

"German agents are active throughout the country. It's the usual TEAM mixture, traders, explorers, archaeologists, and missionaries. They're busy stirring up trouble and preaching sedition.

"We won't be based in Tehran. There's too much politics, it's too far from the southern regions, the Persian Army is actually strong there, and there's little trouble there. We'll be based in the centre of the country, place called Esfahan. Good links with all the trouble spots, and it's got some issues with a weak Army presence and a high level of banditry.

"On the positive side, I've been told to use my own judgement in detailed operational matters. If we do well, the Government will take the credit. If we err, I'll take the blame. However, we will be able to exercise our own judgement. Remember that it's quite likely that your company may be on an independent operation far from support. Any questions?"

*****

"Ma'am, I have request." Frank stood stiffly, trying to hide his nervousness. "Now I am Corporal, I have responsibilities, much to do, and now not able to go off camp. I wish ask you if I can ask Joy to get those railway novels, to help Regiment. Help Persian volunteers learn English also. Be good to get books here soon."

"Corporal Barry, I'm impressed. Promotion, a sense of responsibility, and a scheme to get the outcome you want. Very impressive. I will finish this letter. You may give Joy the news."

Joy was folding cloth over silver in the adjoining room, carefully wrapping the silver.

"I have news," he said. "Rifleman Barry not going to Persia."

Joy's face fell and tears filled her eyes. "But the Regiment is going. I'm going."

"Rifleman Barry not going." Frank held out the stripes. "When I sew these on, I am Corporal Barry."

Joy blinked, puzzled for a moment, and then she realised what Frank was saying, and she gave a squeal of excitement. "You've been promoted? Is Corporal a type of Sergeant?" She laughed with pleasure and flung her arms around him. "That was so cruel a joke, making me think we'd be apart. I should have known better. I love you so much." She sighed and hugged Frank more tightly, then she looked away. "If we can marry when you're a Sergeant, I think becoming a Corporal means you can kiss me."

Frank leaned forward to kiss her gently on the cheek, confused by her asking him to kiss her. Women just didn't initiate such things. That was the man's job. He'd intended to kiss her on the cheek, but somehow it was her lips he was kissing, and he was sure he could feel her heart start to race.

"Duty before pleasure," came Lady Dalkeith's voice from the doorway, a million miles away.

*****

Thomas stood at attention in front of Colonel Dalkeith's desk.

"You wish to speak with me, Lance-Corporal O'Grady?"

"Yes, Sir. Went to a market in London, Sir. Lots of stall, lots of things there. Picked up this book, Sir." That was not a lie. Not really. He had picked it up, just not from the market. "Lady Dalkeith said you liked the author, Sir. Thought you might like the book." He placed the book on the desk.

Colonel Dalkeith didn't touch it, but looked at Thomas. "Was it stolen?"

"No, Sir. Stall owner said he couldn't sell it, said he'd give it to me if I helped him shift some things." That, however, Thomas ruefully admitted to himself, was an outright lie.

"I see." Colonel Dalkeith picked up the book and glanced at a couple of pages. "Scenes of the Mississippi, Fanny Trollope."

"Yes, Sir." Thomas tried to bite his tongue, but it seemed to have a life of its own. "Thought you might like a Trollope for the trip to Persia, Sir." At least he'd kept an expressionless face.

The Colonel's face reddened. "A kind gesture doesn't excuse impertinence, Rifleman."

Thomas glanced at his new stripe.

"Lance-Corporals know how to avoid being grossly impertinent. Promotions can be revoked. Have that stripe taken off and advise Sergeant Taylor that you're not to be promoted again until you learn to control that tongue of yours."

"Sorry, Sir."

"Dismissed."

As he closed the door, Thomas heard the Colonel start to laugh.

*****

The Regiment disembarked from the train. Packs were full to bulging point, and sergeants were shouting themselves hoarse to get the men into some sort of order. The train was going on to the docks with their heavy supplies, and they were standing in the cold morning light at a station that was miles from anywhere.

"Chance for you to stretch your legs," Sergeant Taylor said to the platoon. "You'll not get much chance once we're on the boat. Ten miles to the boat. Make the most of it. Take them out, Corporal Barry."

Frank found himself alongside Lieutenant Hawkins at the head of the platoon as the Regiment marched out of the station and onto a small road winding its way through the countryside. He didn't really have to do anything. There was only one way they could go, he didn't need to call step, or worry about dressing. They'd done route marches dozens of times. This was just one more.

"That's when something comes up," said Lieutenant Hawkins.

"Beg pardon, Sir?"

"When you think everything's under control, that's when something crops up. The trick to staying in control is to keep on top of things."

"Yes, Sir. How did you know, Sir?"

"Experience. It'll come. Drop back, make sure they're carrying their packs properly, keep your eye on them."

"Yes, Sir." Frank started to turn to head back to check up on the men.

"By the way, Corporal, make sure they see that you're checking up on them. It makes them realise they're being checked up on," Lieutenant Hawkins said.

"Yes, Sir." Frank started to head back, determined to make sure the men didn't get into mischief.

Lieutenant Hawkins stopped him. "By the way, Corporal, if they get chance to think, they'll think their way into mischief. If they're singing bawdy songs, they're not going to be thinking of getting into mischief."

"Yes, Sir."

"By the way, Corporal, always remember that you're to be a steadying influence on the men. They'll be looking to you to set an example. Make sure it's a good one."

"Yes, Sir." Frank started to turn yet again, only to pause and try and control a sigh as Lieutenant Hawkins spoke again.

"By the way, Corporal. Word of advice. If your young lady will be on the troopship, make sure that it's public knowledge she's your young lady. If you don't, someone will make advances to her on the trip without realising.

That could lead to unpleasantness. If you do, someone may make advances, but they'll know the risk they're running. Standard rule among the officers is unattached young ladies are fair game, attached young ladies are out of season. She might want to sidestep Lieutenant Furley-Smith. He's one who is not inclined to distinguish."

"Yes, Sir. Thank you for advice, Sir."

"Come on, Corporal. Get started on checking the men."

Frank dropped back and he found that although Sergeant Taylor made it look easy, it wasn't as easy as it seemed to look at the men and walk forwards at the same time. When your head was turned and you were looking away, walking in a straight line wasn't easy. "Get your pack up on your shoulders, O'Grady, not resting on your post area."

"That's posterior, Frank."

"That's Corporal Barry, O'Grady."

"Yes, Corporal Barry O'Grady."

Frank sighed. Why did Thomas always have to answer back? "Lance-Corporal Miller. O'Grady has just volunteered to carry your pack. Give him a reminder if he starts to slack."

That cheered the men up, and after laughing at Thomas' misfortune, they started to sing one of their marching songs.

"We're Riflemen we sing this song,
"Doo dah, doo dah.
"We'll be dead before too long.
"Oh, doo dah day.
"Going to die tonight, going to die today.

"They'll bury my body in an unmarked grave.
"Who cares anyway?"

"The blazing sun will do its worst
"If cholera don't get us first."

The song went on to list the many painful ways soldiers can die on campaign. There were a lot of verses of this cheerful little ditty, and invariably someone would add a new one to it.

"Locked up in a harem's room,
"It makes a very happy tomb.
"Fornicate all night,
"Fornicate all day.
"They'll never get the lid of my coffin down
"My pecker went to town."

It carried them through the miles, with an increasingly bawdy element to it.

"Corporal, populated area," said Lieutenant Hawkins.

"March to attention. That includes you, O'Grady. Give Lance-Corporal Miller's pack back."

They were now marching through the streets leading to the docks. Broad streets and a string of small shops with homes above them, and a lot of pubs. Frank noticed that the other NCOs had positioned themselves between the troops and the pubs.

"No need to move. You're good where you are," said Lieutenant Hawkins. "Your girl's Lady Dalkeith's maid, correct?"

"Yes, Sir," said Frank, wondering how the Lieutenant knew.

"Right, lead them into the docks. Eyes right on passing the Colonel and his entourage, then lead them to the stores on the dock by the ship. We're the lead platoon. Just take it nice and steady and easy."

"Shouldn't you do that, Sir?"

"I've got to speak with Sergeant Taylor about loading the ship. Just focus on the job in hand."

Suddenly, Frank felt very alone. He was at the head of the platoon, and the platoon was at the head of the Regiment, and they were all following his lead. What would happen if he messed up? What if everyone just ran off? What if he got lost and walked around the town in circles? What if they refused to follow him?

Through the gateway and approaching the Colonel. Five paces to go. Was it eyes right or eyes left? Which was left and which was right?

"Eyes right." His voice cracked, and it didn't come out crisp and sharp like Sergeant Taylor did it, and the salute was pretty ragged, but it was done. He saw the Colonel with a sailor, pausing in his talking while the Regiment went past. Lady Dalkeith was with Joy, instructing her in something. Then Lady Dalkeith glanced at the Regiment, spoke to Joy, who looked. She saw him and gave a little squeal, and beamed a huge smile at him, and he had to concentrate on keeping an expressionless face.

"Front," hissed Thomas.

"Front," shouted Frank, hoping no-one had noticed that he'd forgotten. The salute had gone on for far too long, but Joy had seen him. He led the platoon to the dock next to the ship, with an enormous pile of stores and equipment on the dockside.

"Corporal Barry, go and make sure Lady Dalkeith's luggage is taken aboard safely," said Lieutenant Hawkins. "You've got a voyage to practise crisp commands."

*****

The ship wasn't one of the big Royal Navy warships, but an elderly troopship. Thomas read the name: HMT Saltash Castle. About 200 feet long, three funnels, two decks, cabins on the upper decks, and a few temporary-looking buildings. Black and with flecks of soot everywhere. Cranes were loading coal into the hull from barges alongside the ship.

On the dockside was a huge pile of stores and equipment, and Thomas looked at this with bemusement. It would take days to load it all. Crates containing every conceivable thing that might be needed: ammunition and potatoes and spare uniforms and boots and tools, all packaged into hundred-weight loads and crated up, in enormous piles around the rather grubby dock next to the two-decked transport ship that would be their home for the next two months.

"We are going to shift that onto the deck of the ship," explained Sergeant Taylor. "Luckily, you will not need to move from the spot I puts you in. The first man picks up a load and throws it to the second man. He does not catch it. He puts his hands under it and pushes it on to the next man in line. He does the same. Do not catch and stop it, hands under and push it on. Once it gets up the gangway, you starts slowing it down as you push it on, and the last man stacks it. While he's stacking it, the next last man takes his place and catches the next load. You will stand where I put you, and you will not move from that spot, excepting the last men. Any questions?"

"Wouldn't it be easier to carry it on?"

"Just two gangplanks. It would take forever."

"Sergeant, what happens if we misjudge the throw?"

"Then you'll have a hundred-weight of load come crashing into you. If you're in the middle of the line, it will hurt and then I'll have a word with you about damaging Regimental property, and that will hurt as well. It's just a matter of rhythm. O'Grady's Catholic, he'll tell you what rhythm is."

"Sergeant, I'm not Catholic."

"Name like O'Grady, of course you're Catholic. Big strong lad like you will be at the start of the chain, well away from the fast bits. You are a lucky boy."

The Sergeants started placing the men. Thomas was surprised at how far apart the men in the middle were, some ten feet apart. He noticed that the biggest and strongest men were at the ends of the line. Then he picked up the first box, lifted it up, and threw it the foot distance to the next man. It wasn't easy; picking up a crate weighing over one hundred pounds was hard work, and there was a huge stack of them. Bend down to pick up the next box, and pass it on, and get into a rhythm. Bend, pick, pass on.

After a quarter of an hour, someone took his place. He was sweating copiously, and his shoulders and arms ached. Sergeant Taylor even let him smoke while he took a break.

He saw a group of four women in nurses uniform going up the other gangplank.

"Who are they, Sergeant?" he asked.

"Nurses, O'Grady. The Colonel said that disease and illness and wounds going bad kills more men than any enemy, so we got four nurses coming with us. They're civilian non-coms, so don't start getting any ideas."

Thomas watched the nurses, and one of them looked at the soldiers loading the stores. He recognised her, Nurse Charrington. Her red hair was unmistakeable.

"Of course, Sergeant. I won't get any ideas." That, he thought to himself, was a complete lie.